# Praise for the Mead

"One of the freshest voices in fantasy romance! This book has it all: spice, humor, and a world I want to get lost in!"
—Katee Robert, *New York Times* bestselling author

"Sexy, witty, and fun as hell—*That Time I Got Drunk and Saved a Demon* is the instant mood boost we all need."
—Hannah Whitten, *New York Times* bestselling author

"Hilarious, hot, and full of heart, *That Time I Got Drunk and Saved a Demon* is exactly what you need in your life. Right now. Go pick it up because it is the cure to any reading funk and might even clear up acne. I'm serious. It's that good."
—Avery Flynn, *USA Today* and *Wall Street Journal* bestselling author

"A hilarious, down-to-earth romance with magic, adventure, and intrigue. What's not to love?"
—Talia Hibbert, *New York Times* bestselling author

"Perfect entertainment for my stressed-out brain, and I was definitely rooting for those two wacky kids to have their HEA."
—*Smart Bitches, Trashy Books*

## By Kimberly Lemming

### MEAD MISHAPS

*That Time I Got Drunk and Saved a Demon*

*That Time I Got Drunk and Yeeted a Love Potion at a Werewolf*

*That Time I Got Drunk and Saved a Human*

### MEAD REALM NOVELLAS

*Mistlefoe*

*A Bump in Boohail*

# THAT TIME I GOT DRUNK AND SAVED A DEMON

## MEAD MISHAPS: BOOK ONE

### KIMBERLY LEMMING

orbitbooks.net

Copyright © 2021 by Kimberly Lemming
Excerpt from *The Undertaking of Hart and Mercy* copyright © 2022 by Megan Bannen

Cover design by Alexia E. Pereira
Cover art by Mike Pape
Cover copyright © 2024 by Hachette Book Group, Inc.
Map by @Saumyasvision/Inkarnate
Author photograph by Kimberly Lemming

Orbit
Hachette Book Group
1290 Avenue of the Americas
New York, NY 10104
orbitbooks.net

First Orbit Paperback Edition: January 2024
First Orbit Ebook Edition: May 2023
Previously published in paperback in Great Britain by Jo Fletcher Books,
an imprint of Quercus Editions Ltd, in August 2023
Previously published in ebook in Great Britain by Jo Fletcher Books,
an imprint of Quercus Editions Ltd, in March 2023
Originally published in paperback and ebook in August 2021

Orbit is an imprint of Hachette Book Group.
The Orbit name and logo are trademarks of Little, Brown Book Group Limited.

The publisher is not responsible for websites (or their content) that are not owned by the publisher.

The Hachette Speakers Bureau provides a wide range of authors for speaking events. To find out more, go to hachettespeakersbureau.com or email HachetteSpeakers@hbgusa.com.

Orbit books may be purchased in bulk for business, educational, or promotional use. For information, please contact your local bookseller or the Hachette Book Group Special Markets Department at special.markets@hbgusa.com.

Library of Congress Control Number: 2023943530

ISBNs: 9780316570275 (trade paperback), 9780316570268 (ebook)

Printed in the United States of America

LSC-C

Printing 6, 2024

# THAT TIME I GOT DRUNK AND SAVED A DEMON

UBBIN'S
EYE

LEEFSIDE

FOLI

LO   TOSKA

DOVEPORT   VASTUS   SOLIME

VELD

FOOL'S
MARCH

OSWARY

GOLDCREST
CITY

WANDERMERE

MYTHEGLIN

LEGEND

CITY

COUNTRY
LINES

# Content Warning

# Chapter 1

I had only two things on my mind: cheese and how to get home. All around me, people danced and sang to the drunken groove of the village baker laying his soul down on his trusty lute while his wife backed him up with her flute. Drums beat to the rhythm of stomping feet as the village came alive with the Hero's Call festival.

It had been a long time since the goddess Myva called upon one of us lowly humans to join the never-ending battle against the monsters trapped behind Volsog gate. As if by some evil clockwork, the gate would weaken every fifteen years. Every manner of myths and monsters would flood through its passage and wreak havoc from our glittering coasts to the deep harsh mountains of the North, where only the maddest of men lived.

None of that, however, was why we were celebrating. No. The reason for our village-wide riot was the fact that we would finally be rid of the uppity brat that was chosen. Priscilla was a fine girl, if a little full of herself. Until her face appeared in the sacred chalice during the Great Calling. Each time Volsog gate opened, the goddess will shine a light into each of her four temples to call forth her chosen heroes to fight back the demons and close the gate once more. A high honor, to be sure. But everyone loved to conveniently ignore the minor issue of our heroes not always coming back.

It was an honor that I had NO desire to be a part of. I was fine with letting Priscilla and those other fools go off and die. *I'll stick to selling my spices, thank you very much.*

My self-preserving habits made me a bit of an outlier with the other girls in town. "Who wouldn't want to go off on a grand adventure with a bunch of hot heroes also chosen by the goddess?"

*Me, bitches. No, thank you.*

Biceps were nice, but so was not having my guts eaten by an orc.

Nevertheless, the promise of finding love with a handsome hero from another village was more than enough incentive to get many women praying for the day they'd be chosen as Myva's "lucky" winner. Maybe we all just grew up reading too many fairy tales.

Priscilla was one of them. Soon after the chipper blond was

presented with her new role, no one could hear the end of her bragging until it was time to kick her ass out of the village, sword in hand.

*Bye.*

The image brought a sting of the memory of my ex leaving town for similar reasons. My lack of desire to be eaten by orcs was a turnoff, and the bastard needed a more adventurous woman. Weeks of crying later, a dear friend came over to slap me out of my sad-girl routine to remind me that "he ain't shit."

*Who needs him? Or any man! Love is for people with not enough wine in their hands!*

With an equilibrium entirely hampered by my love of wine, I stumbled out of the dancing crowd into the food stalls in my daring quest for more cheese. My trusted nose locked on to the smell of aged cheddar and the race was on. With a mighty step over a passed-out blacksmith, followed by a not so graceful stumble past empty wine bottles, I found myself at the glorious cheese stall owned by my best friend and cheesemaker, Brie. Brilliant name for a cheesemaker, I know. Her mother thought herself wildly clever for that one.

"Brie!" I hollered over the music, slumping my body over the counter. "Brie, my goddess of cheese! Bring me that sweet, sweet Gouda!"

The tarp leading to the back room of the stall opened, revealing my amused friend. Her light pink hair flitted loosely past her shoulders as she stuck her hands on her hips. Her pink locks sent my mind into a stupor until I realized we had agreed to dye our hair pink that morning.

"Cinnamon Hotpepper, you are drunk as a skunk!"

OK, so maybe my mom thought she was terribly clever with names as well.

"Pfft, you look like you dunked your head in a pile of snapdragon," I laughed, eyeing her hair.

She wiped her hands on her apron and fixed me with a glare. "Says the woman who came up with this brilliant idea. What was it you said, O wise one? 'Let's dye our hair pink now that the goddess finally chose her sacrificial lamb.'"

"I may have said something along those lines." I mean, it was true. Brie grabbed one of my pink braids and flipped it out of my face to emphasize her point. "You can't say it didn't work, though. Neither of us was chosen; now we can party!" My friend had always been the logical sort who shared my disinterest in danger and death. We dressed in plain clothing and tried not to stand out in the village to avoid being picked.

It was common knowledge that Myva loved her pretty things. The heroes' party was always made up of two men and two women. Each one was always some beautiful flamboyant nut, not necessarily the best for the job. Sometimes I wondered if Myva just picked them to be entertained. But hey, I'm no goddess, so what do I know?

"Enough with that sour face. Gimme some cheddar to go

with this wine and come drink with me!" Far too impatient to mind manners, I grabbed a slice of cheddar and bit a sizable chunk. Its sharp taste danced across my tongue in time with the baker's lute as I took a swig from my wine glass to help wash it down.

"Cin, my sweet girl, that was a whole-ass mood and not in a good way." She shook her head at me disapprovingly and snatched the glass from my hand. "You're done, hun."

"Lies! I have not yet begun to drink!"

"From the looks of it, you began to drink about four glasses ago. Go home, Cin. I won't be done manning the stall for a few more hours anyway. But tomorrow, it's my brother's turn. If you manage to survive the blinding hangover you're going to have in the morning, then I promise we can make a mess of ourselves for the last day of the festival." My stalwart companion paused her motherly ribbing to package up a few slices of Gouda before handing it to a customer to my side.

"You pr-promise?" I hiccuped.

"I swear on the temple itself. So go home for tonight and sleep it off." Her heart-shaped face turned severe and her coal eyes danced with delight. "For tomorrow, we have two things to celebrate. Freedom from the choosing... and freedom from Priscilla's constant... Priscillaness."

A mug slammed on the table, making us both jump. "Hell, I'll drink to that!" The source of our fright was the blacksmith, John. He was undoubtedly another victim to the princess of self-importance, as he had been tasked with making a suitable weapon for her journey. "If I ever get another request for a periwinkle sword that 'can't be too heavy, but not too frilly' again, I will retire on the spot!" he hollered.

Maybe John had it a little worse than the rest of us.

I gave the older man a pat on the back. "But what a beautiful blade it was! I'm sure it will get our heroine to Goldcrest City without fail."

John smiled and nodded his head in pride. "It is a fine blade if I do say so myself. It took me two entire months to make it." The blacksmith was a gruff fellow but never passed up the chance to talk about his creations.

As much of a pain as our little heroine could be, all of us still wanted her home at the end of her journey. Maybe with a handsome hero in tow. Picturing her getting the fairy-tale ending she always wanted was easier than thinking about her not coming home at all. The chosen heroes had never failed in their quest before. In the end, most of the crazed demons had been killed off or pushed back behind the gate. But I couldn't help but wonder: if the goddess was powerful enough to banish all demons when she first came to this land, why did she need heroes to repeat the action every fifteen years?

Suddenly, an enormous boom shook the earth, knocking us off our feet. Near my family's farm, a gigantic dust cloud plumed in the air off toward the East. The crowd fell silent, aside from a few startled screams. "What in the three hells was that?" John slurred. I scrambled back on my feet, looking around wildly.

"Is everyone OK?" I yelled.

"I'm g-good," Brie stammered.

All around me, villagers looked around worriedly as they dusted themselves off. The baker's booming laugh cut through the thick silence as he helped his wife back on her feet.

"What's all this worry?" he began. With a pat on his lute, he began playing once more. "Can't you lot see? It's our mighty heroine doing her damned duty already! Kill all those damn demons, I say! By the time that firecracker gets to the castle, there won't be any left for the other heroes!"

"Yeah, that must be it. Give 'em the wrath of our goddess, Priscilla!" another man roared, eager to push the thought of terror away. Soon the crowd erupted in cheers of affirmation as the dust settled. All sense of danger dissipated as the other musicians resumed their playing.

Brie looked at me with a worried expression. "I sure hope that's all it was. The smoke cloud looked close to your farm. Is your harvest going to be alright?"

I waved her off with a grin. "Don't you worry about us. We've already brought in most of the fall harvest. If it hit the fields, there's not much left."

"That's good to hear," she said with a sigh. "Still. I think you should head home. You're still looking a bit too sloshed for your own good."

"Yes, mother," I teased, bidding my companions farewell with one last bite of cheese, and heading out of the festival toward home. I grabbed one of the backup torches at the festival entrance and lit it. It was way too dark to travel home by moonlight.

Thankfully, my family's farm was close enough to the village that I could stumble my way back with enough booze in my system to kill a moose.

I know; I've done it a dozen times or so.

Food stalls and lantern lights gave way to winding trees and glittering night stars. The spirited music died off in the distance. A bit creepy, honestly. All I could hear were my footsteps crunching the leaves beneath my feet and the crackle of fire from the torch. It was so quiet I could hear myself think. Which is not ideal. Thinking leads to worrying and worrying leads to—

"WHAT THE GINGER WAS THAT SOUND?!"

I whipped around to see a squirrel darting up in a tree. The little critter stopped to eye me for a moment before skittering up into the trees above. "Oh. Of course, it was just a squirrel. What else would it be?" The all-encompassing crunch of the leaves resumed as I swallowed my paranoia and kept going. My home was only a two-mile walk. The blast from earlier probably just fried my nerves a bit.

As if on cue, some twat in a black tartan and a matching scarf to cover his face jumped out before me.

Clearly, the gods had favorites, and I wasn't one of them.

He brandished a relatively small hammer and pointed at my person.

I threw my head back and sighed heavily.

"Give me your valuables, wench, and no one gets hurt," the bandit said.

"Wench? Shut the hell up. Who are you, my grandpa? No one talks like that."

The masked man barely stood taller than me, yet still dared to stomp his foot impatiently, and raised his hammer higher. "OK fine, whatever," he grunted. "Just give me your coins before I get pissed off."

"What coins? I don't have coins. I should rob you! I'm a farmer, dickhead. Everyone in this area is a fucking farmer!" Not exactly true; my family made nice money off of our cinnamon harvest. Primarily because we are the only ones who grow it... cause we won't tell anyone else how to grow it. But hey, ya gotta make your own way in this world.

Not that some fool trying to mug me needed to know that.

"I like your cloak. Cough it up," he said.

"You have a cloak on you. What do you want mine for anyway? You mean this green one with the yellow sunflower pattern down the rim?" I gave it a twirl to show off the pretty pattern my little cousin Angelica hemmed for me last fall. "You really think you can pull off this look? I don't know, man, seems kind of suss."

"Just give me the clothes, woman!"

"You freaking bandits just be doing this shit for the giggles! Are you that bored? Go to the festival and get drunk like a normal person!"

"Give me the damn cloak, woman!"

"You can't pull off this look, bro. You can barely pull off that tattered scarf falling off your face."

The bandit yanked the scarf back up to fully cover his face. But not before I glimpsed red hair peeking past freckled cheeks. Humph. No surprise, it would be one of the Huckabee boys. Mr. Huckabee was a fisherman with five boys and no wife to keep them in line. So it fell to the rest of the village and me to smack them around from time to time. If not, their shenanigans would drive us all mad. "Maybe I'm not going to use it for myself! Have you ever thought of that? I'll uh...I'll give it to my girlfriend!"

"Harper," I began, putting my free hand on my waist. "Look at me. You do not have a girlfriend. I don't know who you're trying to fool right now."

His eyes went wide, and I could just picture his stupid open-mouthed face as he took in my retort. "I'm not Harper! I'm just a roaming bandit. You're mean!"

"You're trying to ROB me!" The metal of the hammer in his hand reflected the moonlight as it caught my eye. "Harper, I swear to the goddess I will shove this torch where the sun doesn't shine," I said, grasping the torch with two hands and giving it a test swing in his direction.

Harper lowered the hammer and cocked his head to the side as he took in the situation. Then, slowly, he lifted his hands and backed away slightly. "You know what, I'm feeling generous. Imma let you go this time. We'll just forget this whole thing."

"Yeah, I don't think so, fish-boy. How about you give me your cloak?" I took a step toward him and raised the torch higher.

"Naw, Cin, you don't need this old thing. Just go on home."

"Ah-ha!" My shout could have raised the dead, but I was way too drunk to care. "How do you know my name is Cin if you're just a roaming bandit?"

"Crap."

"Yeah, I got you now! Gimme that cloak!"

I darted toward him, but he turned tail and ran off into the woods. Without a second thought, I chased in after him. Why? I wasn't too sure. I didn't want his cloak. But I was sick of his shit. It was always one thing or another with those boys. If nothing else, stealing his cloak would let me get back at them for the time they tramped through my chili pepper fields with no regard for how long it took me to grow them. Such audacity had to be corrected.

Harper was always a fast kid, but my drunken need for this vendetta propelled me forward, stumbling over pretty much every rock and branch that got in the way.

His black attire made him hard to see in the darkness, and

soon I couldn't quite tell which way he went. Finally, following my gut, I steered left at a giant oak tree, hoping to catch up to him.

A weak groan cut through the silence of the night, so I veered toward it full force, blood pumping in my ears.

Instead of my wannabe bandit, I came across the aftermath of what appeared to be a rock slide: trees were splintered into nothing, as giant piles of rocks made a scar across the land. I guess that would explain the enormous boom at the festival. Whatever demon that had disturbed Priscilla's path must have caused this damage. Hopefully, our little heroine was able to leave unscathed.

My thoughts were brought into focus as another weak groan cut through the night air. Panic rose in my chest. If a villager had been caught in the landslide during the battle, they could have been seriously injured.

"Where are you?" I called. "Keep making noise so I can find you."

I looked around for any sign of Harper. If I took the time to go back to the village for help, whoever was trapped might be crushed before I made it back.

A low cough sounded to my right, and I carefully climbed over the rocks and rubble until I grew closer to the sound.

"I'm here," a weak voice called. Several branches covered a slumped form, but I could see a pale hand poking out from the mess. Whoever it was could count themselves lucky that it was just branches covering him and not the boulders. I'm no pushover, but I'm no ox either.

"Don't worry, stranger, I got you," I said, coming to his side. My torch flickered when I placed it between two rocks to free both my hands. Carefully, I removed the branches from the man. Midback-length black hair hid his face from me, and he seemed much larger than anyone I knew from my village. Must have been some kind of vagabond. No one around Boohail had hair that long. We didn't get too many travelers. Maybe his hometown had been overrun by demons, and he had left to find help.

Tough luck on his end. I only hoped whatever he was running from didn't make it to Boohail—though demons invading wasn't something we needed to worry about so close to the village. Myva's temple held a powerful shield most monsters couldn't get through. Its reach spanned far enough outside our town that we would live in relative peace, even when Volsog gates opened.

I slowly ran my hands over his form, checking to see if I could find any broken bones or large wounds. His frock was in tatters. But other than that, he seemed like he'd live. "Are you hurt? Can you stand?"

"I'm feeling drained, to be honest." The stranger's deep voice sent a pleasant thrill down my spine. He sat up beside me as I knelt next to him, supporting his weight. *Holy crows, this man is big!* Even sitting down, his frame towered over mine.

I brushed some of the long hair out of his face, noticing how his pale skin contrasted against my dark brown complexion. The sun beat down here in Kinnamo like we owed it money. The fact that the man wasn't as red as a lobster was surprising. As my wrist moved past his mouth, he gave a small sigh. Maybe it was the alcohol, perhaps it was my paranoia, but I could have sworn I saw twin fangs peek out behind his pale lips. I cleared my throat to stop my mind from racing. "You got some pretty bad luck to be caught up in this mess. Did you see what happened?"

The man made a strangled sound as his body began to shake. "As a matter of fact, I did. Unfortunately, however, you're The Unlucky One in this situation. I'm afraid you'll need to grab your torch and run. It's poor form to let your savior die."

"...What?"

Yellow eyes glowed beneath a halo of ink-black hair. The stranger shook more brutally as a low growl rolled past his lips. "RUN!" he bellowed, whipping his head to look up at me. In the dim light of the torch flame, his pupils slid into cat-like slits, his colossal frame shaking even harder.

The air was suddenly gone from my lungs. A second later, I realized it was because a large hand was wrapped around my throat as the man-*demon* hoisted me off the ground. My feet kicked out, trying to dislodge him, but I may as well have been trying to push a boulder off me. A popping noise caught my attention, and I looked up to see horns as they grew out of the top of my assailant's head. They curved back behind him before turning forward and twisting back again. They formed an S shape that was wide at the base, then tapered off into sharp daggers, serrated and full of malice. I did not doubt that they could rip the skin right off a man.

"Oh...fuck no." My Fight or Flight response kicked into overdrive. No way in hornet's nest was I planning to die there. I clutched the torch tightly in my hand and slammed the fiery end directly into his face.

The creature roared and dropped me to clutch at its burning face. Immediately I took off running. I doubted that I'd ever be able to outrun a freaking demon, of all things, but I did have the home advantage. My family's cinnamon fields were a complete maze to a stranger, and right then, that was the best hope I had. My breath came out in a ragged wheeze. I forced air back into my lungs and ran. Behind me, I could hear the demon let loose an angry chorus of roars as it tore through the foliage behind me. I jumped between two trees growing close together in the hopes that it would slow him down and veered to my right, praying I would reach the fields in time.

To my horror, a loud boom shot off behind me, followed by the crackle and groan of trees falling. Did...did this fool just smash his way through TREES?!

"I am so fucked," I muttered into the chilly night.

Putting all my hopes and dreams into my legs, I ran faster.

The smell of cinnamon called back to me like a goddamn savior as I reached the fields. I dove through several of the small trees as I zig-zagged around the maze. Then, finally, the demon's angry shouts quieted down.

*Did he lose sight of me?*

Far too much of a coward to look back, I kept going further until I reached the middle of the field. In the distance, I could hear Mr. Snarls-A-Lot shuffling around, no doubt lost. As quietly as possible, I settled down amidst a cluster of cinnamon trees. My body shook like a leaf as I tried to control my breathing. Fuck, fuck, fuck, FUCK! How does that shit even happen? The whole point of putting up with that brat Priscilla was so the Chosen One could deal with crap like this before it came back to bite the rest of us!

OK. That was probably really unfair to her, but still: how powerful was that freak to push past Myva's barrier?

After a few minutes, I could no longer hear the demon shuffling around at the edge of the field.

*Did he give up? Or better yet, did the asshole die of his injuries?*

One could hope.

Slowly, I shifted my weight down to my stomach and crawled out towards my parents' home. Our land spanned about four hundred acres, divided between my two brothers, myself, and my mom and pa. Unfortunately, my section was on the other side of the freaking property, the one time my stupid butt tried to help a demon. So the best solution was to do what any grown woman should do in her time of need: run home to mommy and daddy.

The bark of the cinnamon trees scraped up my tunic as I crawled slowly forward. A twig caught the hem of my cloak, and I swear to the goddess the rip that ensued was the loudest thing on this side of the country.

I froze. The thump of my heartbeat sounded like a thousand drums in my ears, but I heard nothing else. Crickets chirped their cares away while fireflies mulled about.

"Is he gone?" I got up from my stomach and took off in a sprint for my pa's house, veering left and right in a maze I grew up in. The deeper I drove into the fields, the more hopeful I became. I chanced a look behind me, half expecting a clawed hand to reach out and snatch me. But it was nothing but more cinnamon trees.

A hysterical giggle ripped past my lips as I grew closer to my destination. I covered my mouth with my hands while I ran to keep down the frantic laughter building. The green roof of my parents' home came into view right when a thought crossed my mind: When had the crickets stopped chirping? A sudden weight crashed into my side and my head hit the ground. Above me were the haunting yellow eyes of a predator. His large hands pinned my shoulders to the ground, and his lips pulled back to reveal sharp fangs. "Can't..." I gasped to get the air back into my lungs. "Can't we talk this through? I can get you a great deal on some spices. My family's farm is top-notch!"

The demon snarled and one clawed hand moved to my throat and squeezed.

"OK, not a spice guy, I get it." I was rambling at that point, but I really couldn't stop if I tried. I reached out for anything I could use as a weapon. My fingers grazed a fallen branch just within reach. I inched my hand closer, trying to grab hold. "Listen, we don't farm much meat. I can offer you some choice goats if meat is more your style." My vision darkened, but I used the last of my strength to snatch the branch and bring it up as hard as I could to smash it against his face. The overpowering smell of cinnamon stung my nose as the branch broke against his face. The demon snarled and rolled off me to rub at his nose. I stumbled to my feet and shot off to the front door.

Without looking back this time, I busted into my parents' home and locked the door shut. Then I scrambled over to the wooden kitchen table and dragged it to block the door.

My body collapsed against the makeshift barrier as I tried to catch my breath.

"FFFFFFUCK!"

# Chapter 2

Needless to say, I didn't get that much sleep that night. My parents woke up to find me piling half their things in front of the door and decided the smell of wine meant their daughter was a drunken mess and demanded I sleep it off. I must have spent hours peeking through windows before Ma gave up, threw a pillow at my head, and went back to bed. The night crept on with no sign of my attacker until the sun shone through my ma's immaculately clean windows.

The apple-embroidered curtains lit up with morning light while songbirds mocked me with their optimistic greeting of the day. A fucking demon attacked me last night, and the day had the audacity to shine as if nothing happened?

*Rude.*

My eyes felt heavy, and I struggled to keep them open. As

much as I tried to fight it, my head dropped. Maybe Ma was right? I was so tired, maybe I did just get too drunk. With a groan, I got up from my guarding spot at the window and made my way over to the guest bed. If Mr. Snarls-A-Lot was real, he didn't seem intent on coming back. With a flop, my head sunk into the pillow like a long-lost friend. Demons and goddess shit should be left to the Chosen One. I was just the Tired One, so I'd leave it at that.

"Ooh, watch out, Cin! I'm a scary demon!" my older brother Cumin shouted, kicking in the door to the guest room. I sighed heavily and rolled over, bringing the pillow over my head to ignore him. "Leave me alone, Cu," I muttered.

The sudden weight on the bed meant I was completely ignored. "No can do, sissy poo!"

"Sissy what?!" I snarled, smacking him upside the head with a pillow. It gave a satisfying whack as his long dreadlocks whipped back from the force of the blow. Cumin raised his arm up in defense, smirking at his stupid nickname.

"Mercy, you bog witch!" The spry little shit jumped up to avoid more of my assault. He wore his everyday field clothes, a simple off-white tunic with mud-stained brown pants. It must have meant he had no plans of bringing our goods to the market today. Strange, as it went on every weekend.

What even was the time? I was so tired. I brought a hand up to rub my sore eyes.

"Listen, I think Pa's taken your drunken tale a little too

20

seriously. So he sent for Chili and me to take you to Myva's temple to ask for protection."

I groaned. At least someone had enough sense to believe me. Our pa always had been an overly cautious one. The goddess' temple lay on the outskirts of Boohail. It was more of a cave that housed the goddess Myva's sacred grail, but it got the job done. The holy power that seeped from the cave was enough to keep any demons away from it—so asking the goddess for help wasn't a bad idea at all. I thought about bringing a few sweets as an offering. It wasn't often my family went to the temple, aside from the occasional holiday, so we'd usually bring a few treats that might sweeten my plea.

"But can it wait till after a nap?" I asked.

"Sure," he replied in that easy tone of his. "I'm stuck in the village anyway. That earthquake from yesterday knocked a few trees onto the main road. So I won't be able to make my market trips until they clear it."

"That explains the work clothes," I said.

"Welp, since you feel the need to sleep the day away, I'll be taking your cinnamon rolls then!" Cumin tore the pillow from its casing as I sprang up, then pulled the pillowcase over my head and shot out of the room to the kitchen.

I stumbled out of bed, tripping over the covers in my haste to chase after him. "You donkey's ass! Those are MINE!" The sound of his cackling could be heard throughout the entire house.

"I hope you choke on it," I muttered, shambling into the kitchen.

"Young lady, no wishing death on your brothers," Ma chided as if we were all still younglings clinging to her apron. Her apple apron had ripped frills and stains for days, but my ma refused to ever get rid of it. When my siblings and I were little, we all pitched in to embroider her signature apples on to the simple white fabric. Most of the apples are lopsided, easily identifiable as children's work, but she loved it all the same. I often wondered if one reason she refused to let it go was its reminder of Cherry. My little sister's empty placemat at my side of the table still felt heavy, even after four years. Try as I might, the empty space remained a constant reminder of what happened when you stepped out of the goddess' protection.

Ma's head was recently shaved, showing off the sharp lines of the tribal tattoos adorning her skull. They were a beautiful remnant of the Scarlet Thorn tribe she hailed from. The bold red ink gave a fierce undertone to her usually friendly demeanor. Barbed thorns wrapped around her skull like a picture frame, while the pattern in the center told the legend of a fierce warrior woman and a werewolf who fought off a massive kraken together. My sister and I would beg her for stories of her homeland in the Far West as kids. Her tales were always of Old Gods in a land lush with adventure and monsters. Sometimes the heroes were fighting with the monsters, others against them. The tales came from before madness took over all demons. Before Myva rose up to save us with her gate. Cherry and I often dreamt of the day where we'd go beyond the bayou of our home and find adventure ourselves. It was an idiot child's dream with deadly consequences. I shook my head to clear my depressing thoughts.

One look at the breakfast feast was enough to have me drooling. There was no point in staying upset when food was on the table. Fresh cinnamon rolls, flapjacks, eggs, and bacon were laid out for a full-on family feast. I wasn't too surprised that Ma would go all out. It wasn't often all of us got together for a meal after my siblings and I reached adulthood.

"I'm too tired to plot Cumin's downfall anyway." The smell of baked goods rolled off my plate like a saucy temptress, one I was content to let lift my foul mood. As if time sped forward, the cinnamon rolls were gone. The only proof of their existence was the frosting around my mouth.

Cumin blinked at me. "Cin," he began, placing his hand on mine and looking at me with deep concern in his eyes. "You don't have to shovel your food anymore. We adopted you from those raccoons when you were a bab—"

My sharp flick to his forehead cut off his words.

Across the table, Pa choked a laugh around his coffee. He never said much—Pa was always content to just sit around and watch the chaos of his family. I liked to think he balanced out his exuberant wife. My brother Chili seemed to take after him the most. Their tall, quiet presence was an easy source of comfort when the rest of the family got too rowdy and annoying. Cumin was usually annoying.

"Where did your demon fella run off to?" Chili spoke up over his bacon and eggs.

"Assuming he even exists, and she wasn't just drunk off her ass. ACK!" The Loud One yelped as I flicked him again.

My fork dug into his plate, scooping up a large piece of his bacon so I could gobble it up to add insult to injury. "I wasn't drunk enough to make up a whole attack!"

"So just half an attack then?"

Ma swore, pointing her wooden spatula like a blade. "Chili! I mean, Cumin! I mean Cinnamon! Dammit, the middle child! Stop badgering the girl child!"

Pa spilled more coffee on his shirt before doubling over in laughter. My brothers and I looked at her incredulously before roaring along.

"Notice how she got it right on the second try, then kept going!" I giggled.

"Then reduced us to birth order!" Cumin roared, doubling over in a fit of laughter.

Chili did his best to regain a straight face and slammed his fist on the table. "Spare male child! Listen to your ma!" he ordered, his face breaking into a grin.

"SPARE MALE CHILD," I wheezed, trying not to choke on my stolen bacon.

The spare male threw himself on the table in a fit of drama.

"Is that all I am to you, mother?! A spare in case Chili perishes in the Great War?"

Ma eyed him with the most deadpan face I'd ever seen in all my twenty-four years. "Yes."

This sparked another laughing fit around the table. Ma smiled at us all and fixed herself a plate. With all of us out of the house and looking after our parts of the family spice business, mornings like these, laughing and sitting around the table, were few and far between. Chili was already pushing thirty and courting a pretty lass in town. With any luck, our family would grow again soon. Ma was constantly hounding us for grandkids, but Cumin and I would rather leave that task to our eldest brother. Cumin was too busy chasing skirts in his travels to nearby towns, and well...I just wasn't ready to even think about kids. I knew plenty of other twenty-four-year-old women who were already on their second or third child, but I couldn't imagine doing it myself.

"But honestly, Cin," Chili spoke again, "if you truly saw a demon, then we need to gather men from the village and find it immediately. Can you tell me what it looked like?"

With my mouth too full of bacon, I held up a finger to him so I could finish chewing before answering.

"I look a bit like this," came a voice outside the kitchen window. The deep voice of my darkest nightmare made me choke on the food I was eating. Bacon grease dribbling down my chin, I turned toward the window to see a tall, lean body resting casually against the open frame. The demon's shoulders were massive and his hips narrow. Why in Goddess' name did I ogle the man who attacked me?

His dark brows furrowed as he cocked his head to the side. "Did the raccoons teach you table manners as well?" A smirk spread across his lips. "You do know the food stays inside your mouth? Waste is an awful thing."

Fear crept up my spine, the memories of last night resurfacing. Why the gods felt the need to bless such a deadly creature with such a beautiful face was beyond me. Instead of the yellow cat-like eyes of last night, the man in the window had dark coal eyes that sucked you into their endless abyss. His hair, black and straight, moved gently in the morning breeze like the leaves on a willow tree. It fell past his shoulders as the light of day danced across his upsettingly handsome face. If it weren't for the large curved horns twisting up from his head, one would think he was just a normal man.

However, the horns were pretty hard to miss.

The demon left the window to let himself in through the front door, ducking his head to avoid hitting his horns. He looked around at my slack-jawed family before settling his gaze on my mother. He took in her tattooed head for a moment and relaxed his shoulders slightly. "Good morning, bard," he said politely. "I'd like to have a word with your girl child."

Chaos ensued. Pa leaped from his chair to push Ma behind him. My brothers ran to the kitchen counter to grab knives from our ma's favorite mahogany knife rack. Chili hollered at the demon to leave and moved to stand in front of me.

Like an idiot, I sat dumbfounded at the table. I was unable to move once the predator in the window fixed his dark gaze on me. The demon didn't move during the chaos of my father shielding my mother and my brothers brandishing sharp weapons in his direction. He didn't even flinch at the danger he was in. My eyes widened in realization as Chili prepared to strike.

He wasn't moving because he was in no danger!

"Chili, stop!" I screamed, reaching for him. However, my reaction speed was too slow. My brother shot out to stab the demon in the chest.

Finally, the predator's gaze shifted off me. Then, in a flash, he struck out at his attacker.

My gut rolled.

Chili flew to the other side of the kitchen and hit the ground with a sickening thud.

Ma screamed and ran to his side as Cumin and Pa took a step back.

For a bone-chilling moment, I thought my eldest brother had died until he began gasping and coughing air back into his lungs.

I let go of a breath I didn't know I was holding.

"Your bravery is commendable but foolish." The intruder brushed a bit of dirt off his coat before sighing as if he was exasperated at our attempts to hold up his day. "I'm not here to fight you. I need to know what this is," he said, holding up a handful of sticks.

Pa squinted at the offered hand. "That's...just some sticks from one of our cinnamon trees," he said. "Who the hell are you?! Why do you care about spice?"

"Ah. How rude of me," the demon chuckled. "My name is Fallon Ozul from the Frost Mountains of Volsog." He put a fist over his chest and bowed slightly before my pa.

I gasped at the level of audacity. "A bit late for a polite introduction, don't you think?" I snapped at him. "You just threw my brother across the room!"

"Would it have been more polite to let him gut me? I admit I'm unfamiliar with human customs, but I doubt your greetings are that extreme."

I rose and pointed a finger at him. "You tried to kill me last night!"

"Semantics." He shrugged.

Pa held out a hand to silence me before I could shoot back at the arrogant son of a bitch. "Why and how are you here?" he asked. "The magic from the goddess' temple has kept you demons out of our village for generations! How did you slip past?"

Fallon raised an eyebrow at my pa and broke out in

laughter. "Goddess?!" he roared. "You think that damn lich is a goddess?!"

*What the hell is a lich?* "Why is this so funny to you? Tell us how you got past the divine magic!" I shouted.

The demon composed himself abruptly, halting mid-chuckle. "This is brilliant," he said, shaking his head. "She's fooled the entire human realm into guarding her phylactery."

"Phy-what?" Cumin asked, clearly confused. But, boy, he wasn't the only one.

Fallon cleared his throat and raised his hands in a placating manner. "Clearly, we've got a lot to talk about. May I sit?" He gestured to the table politely.

This seemed to trigger some profound hostess nature in my ma, who got up from my brother's side. "Of course," she said, pulling out a chair. Pa looked at his crazy wife, but she swatted his gaze away. "Unless you want to end up on the floor next to your son, I suggest we hear the nice man out!" Her tone left no room for argument. Judging by the pained look on Chili's face, I couldn't say I blamed her. Fighting this creature would only lead to more injuries...or worse.

"Rosa—" But Pa was cut off by another wave from Ma before she began fixing her new guest a plate.

Fallon gave her a small smile before taking his seat. The way the demon seemed to defer to her was strange. His large body dwarfed the wooden chair, and it creaked under his weight. The men in my family were reasonably tall compared to the other men in the village, but this demon made each of them look like shrimps. He eyed the food suspiciously, but picked up a piece of bacon and took a test bite. His eyes widened in surprise. He took another bite and began digging into his plate. "This is fantastic, thank you. I can't remember the last time I had a home-cooked meal."

I don't know what asshole taught this man the magic words to my ma's heart, but her eyes sparkled in pride and she sat down and joined him at the table. "Cumin, help your brother up. The rest of you, come sit!" she demanded. "No sense in kicking up a fuss if we don't have to." Ma gave Fallon a polite smile before offering him a cup of coffee.

*What the hell is happening?*

Slowly, I took my chair and sat, watching the demon that tried to kill me the night before…eat breakfast at the family table as if nothing happened. "So, um, Fallon…about last night?"

"Yes, I need to apologize for that," he said, wiping his mouth. "You see, your goddess," he said, making quotation marks with his hands, "…has a neat little trick where she causes my kind to go insane whenever she feels the need for it. For some reason, when you struck me with this cinnamon stick," he explained, sounding out the word for the spice, "it allowed me to regain consciousness, and I'd like to know why."

"So when you went crazy last night after I helped you up?"

Fallon sipped his coffee and nodded. "I'd fallen under the thrall of her spell again. The next thing I remember was waking up while trying to wipe this cinnamon out of my nose."

Pa stared at Fallon wide-eyed. "We've been growing a monster repellent this whole time?"

"Repellent, no, as I can still hold it. However, it does seem to negate the effects of that lich's spell."

Chili sat in his chair with a heavy thump, put a fist on the table, and tried to steady his breath. "You keep saying that word; what is a lich?"

"An undead sorcerer who specializes in necromancy," he answered. "The one you call Myva used to be a powerful witch, and she used that power to put her soul in a phylactery. The only way to kill a lich is to break it."

Ma gasped at him. "That...can't be right! Myva is a goddess."

Fallon smiled ruefully. "Yes, I'm sure it benefits her to have you think that. Around six hundred years ago, she enraged a few rather powerful demons. They tried to kill her after she sacrificed their children to feed her dark magic. She used her newfound power to hypnotize most of the demon population and forced us to migrate to a frozen wasteland, then created Volsog gate to keep us from leaving. From the looks of it, her next step was to pass herself off as a goddess. You've been unknowingly guarding her heart for generations."

Cumin stood up from his chair and glared at Fallon. "Why should we trust anything a demon says? This all sounds insane!"

Our guest sighed and leaned back into his chair. "You don't have to believe what I tell you." He shrugged. "But you can see it for yourself." Fallon reached into his pocket and pulled out a glowing amulet. In its center was a red stone surrounded by smaller green gems. The red stone seemed to pulse in and out like a heartbeat in his hand. He placed the amulet on the table and scooted it over to me. He took a deep breath and exhaled. The large curved horns adorning his head receded into his hair, and his pointed ears curved off to become more human-like.

"That," he said, pointing to the amulet. "Is a charm capable of increasing a demon's power. It also makes us incapable of hiding what we truly are. If you don't believe me, take it and throw it into your goddess' temple."

I picked up the glowing amulet and studied it. "Why are you telling us this? What is your end goal?"

"Perceptive for a human, I like it," he praised. "Now that I've got my wits about me, I'm going to kill that damn woman and put a stop to her ridiculous pandemonium. Every fifteen years she causes my kind to go mad and kill each other. We've been at the mercy of her magic for too long, and it's time to collect on her due."

"But that doesn't explain why you're trying to prove this

to us. You're already strong enough to make it through her magic; you've proven that by coming here. So why not just go to the temple and break the phylactery yourself?"

"Oh, believe me, I tried last night after you ran away. The closer I got, the more crazed I became, even with your cinnamon in my pocket. Her magic was still too strong inside the temple. So I'm here to have you go," he said, pouring himself another cup of coffee.

Red flags shot off in my mind. "Oh no. No, no, no, no, no! I don't do adventures. This has nothing to do with me. Go find somebody with a sword!"

Fallon rested his head on his hand and looked at me like a cat eyeing a mouse. "I'm not asking you to fight a witch. I'm telling you to take the amulet, throw it into the temple to see what that goddess really is, and then break her little cup. Simple."

"But if she breaks the goblet, won't monsters be able to storm our village?" Pa asked.

"The demons in this area wouldn't dare come near your little village if I put my claim on it. Which I will, as I will owe you a favor." He glanced over at me again. "Help me, and your family will be safe. Demons always settle their debts." Fallon put a fist over his chest and looked back at my pa. "You have my word."

"And if she doesn't?" Chili asked.

Fallon smiled, showing very sharp-looking canines. "Then

33

I may just drop the cinnamon from my pocket. I don't think you'll want to see what happens after that. Your bard should have a slew of stories on how difficult fighting my kind is."

"Bard?" I asked.

He nodded toward my ma. "Storyteller, troubadour, whatever humans call them these days. Isn't that what her tattoo signifies? I thought all Scarlet Thorns were bards."

I swallowed hard and looked at my ma. Instead of answering him, I could see her mind running through various scenarios of how to get all of her babies out of here. But deep down, I knew no scheme could save us from fighting off a demon strong enough to push past Myva's barrier.

My hand shook around the amulet. "Fine," I said, glaring at him. "I'll go break your stupid cup."

# Chapter 3

High arches loomed over me as I stood at the entrance to the temple. The demon had stopped at the base of the hill where the temple resided, refusing to go any further. The amulet was cool in my hand, as if the absence of its master had finally subdued its beating heart.

"I just have to throw it in. Just one simple task, and this is all over. I'll see what the goddess truly is. What if something comes out and attacks me? This is all because I dyed my hair pink, isn't it? The one time I decided to stand out, and I get punished for it? Now I have to be some stupid chosen one on a silly quest? This is so unfair. I'm meant to lead a simple life, not do errands for some demon!" There was a good chance I looked like a mad woman muttering to herself, but I was too stressed out to care.

"No, it's no use thinking like that. This will be over as soon as the job is done! All I have to do is break a stupid little cup."

Without giving myself a chance to second-guess this stupidity further, I ran past the stone arches of the entrance and threw the amulet inside. Before it hit the ground, the red stone began pulsing and beating again. It stopped mid-air, then slowly rose higher and higher until its red light shone throughout the goddess' home. The light illuminated a granite altar and a simple wooden goblet.

Every solstice, the village held a feast to honor its owner and the protection she gave us from the monsters that slept beyond Volsog gate in exchange for our loyalty and offerings. "That demon has to be lying. The goddess loves and protects us...doesn't she?" But Fallon's words rang in my head. Could Myva really be the cause of the demons going mad? I had always thought my ma's stories of the time before Myva were just that. Stories. If we really used to live alongside demons, then Myva couldn't be a goddess. She'd be a monster.

All around me, the walls creaked and groaned, and black sludge leaked out of the goblet. I covered my nose and tried not to gag at the putrid scent of rotting flesh permeating the room.

"What in the three hells was that? Fallon was telling the truth!" My fists shook at my sides. Tears built up in the corners of my eyes as the awful truth smacked me in the face. "That slippery snake of a goddess was a liar! All these years worshiping her, sending our people to fight off the monsters SHE drove insane. You gotta be freaking kidding me!"

More sludge and crimson blood poured out of the goblet, as anger burned my chest. The ever-growing pool of sludge and blood on the floor formed two lumps of eyes. More of the sludge formed into a lopsided mouth, screaming in anger. The piercing voice of an angry woman screeched intangible threats as her mouth continued to develop. After seconds of gurgling and screaming, words finally began to form.

"Who...are...you? WHAT HAVE YOU DONE?!"

"I should ask you the same thing, you damned witch!" I said, picking up the blood-covered goblet and smashing it on the ground. The creature screeched in pain when the goblet cracked, but the rest remained intact.

I snatched it up again as a skeleton hand grabbed my ankle and squeezed. I cried out in pain and kicked at where I thought a head would be. Looking back, the arm was attached to absolutely nothing, just a gross skeleton arm clutching my ankle for dear life. Or death. Whatever. "Let go of me, you lying hag!" I screamed. Pain fueled my anger, and I bashed the goblet against the altar. More bones rolled out of the sludge forming themselves into a giant skeletal body with a club made of what looked like a group of femurs tied together by sinew.

The horrid creature groaned and lifted its arm to bash its weapon into my back. I screamed and tried to roll out of the way, but the skeletal arm still held me in place. Before the club could meet its mark, the flash of a sword cut through the chaos and sliced off the offending arm from the undead ogre. I looked up to see Fallon facing off against the putrid beast.

Grinning ear-to-ear, my savior swung his sword again, moving so fast my eyes couldn't catch him. The skeleton ogre fell into pieces around me, its bones clattering on the ground.

"Are you going to lie there all day, or are you going to finish the job?" Fallon asked, glancing back.

For a moment, I hesitated. Was I just trading one horror for another? What would stop him from killing me after he got what he wanted?

"You're shaking like a rabbit trapped in a snare," he chuckled. In a swift motion, he flicked the blood off his sword and turned to face me. "What's wrong? Do you plan on scurrying back in your hole, or are you going to take revenge for all the wrongs this filthy lich has wrought you?" His eyes were back to that unworldly yellow. In the dim light of the temple, they shone with primal joy.

Joy that felt oddly…contagious.

"Take your revenge," the demon insisted. "This lump of undead flesh has been taking advantage of you and yours for generations. Aren't you tired of being used? Won't it feel good to get back at her?"

I kicked away the skeleton arms and stood up, clutching the remains of the goblet. Over his shoulder, I could see the weakening sludge of the false goddess. She gargled more unintelligible nonsense as more bones and blood tried to form into yet another creature. I looked back at Fallon, who was eyeing me intently—as if he was searching my soul to find something buried deep.

"Don't you just want to go feral?"

My breath came out in a harsh shudder and adrenaline coursed through me. Grabbing the goblet by the base, I slammed the tip against the corner of the altar with all the strength I had. Finally, it shattered completely. I dropped to my knees as an ear-splitting screech echoed throughout the temple. The walls shook and cracked and rocks tumbled from the ceiling.

"Fallon, look out!" I shouted before slamming into him, knocking us both to the side before a boulder could smash into his head.

Strong arms wrapped tightly around my waist as the world rushed by me. My stomach churned at the force of it, but the next thing I knew, I was outside the temple, in the safety of the surrounding trees. The temple I once visited every solstice as a child heaved and collapsed onto itself. "It's…it's done." I breathed. Ass-whooping alligators, I actually did it!

My companion barked out a laugh and held me tighter. "I wasn't sure you had the guts, little Rabbit."

A masculine scent of blackcurrant and violet came over me as I noticed just how close we were. The cage of his arms was all too easy to fall into. No doubt it would be a welcome reprieve from the undead ogre and rotting flesh. I sighed and leaned closer to inhale his scent.

*Cin, focus! He could still turn on you!*

Shaking my head, I pushed away from him. "Well, you certainly gave me enough motivation."

"Ah. Right. Humans and their precious families," he said casually, moving over to inspect the rubble.

"You gave your word that they'd be safe!"

"And they will," he replied. "Know this, little Rabbit, I make good on my threats, but I make good on my promises too."

I let out a breath and collapsed onto the ground. "Thank goodness. Well, I wish you the best of luck with the other three temples," I said, waving to him. "Then, if it's all the same to you, I'm going back home."

The smart move would have been to get away from him soon before I got even crazier ideas about that too-handsome face, that stupid, glorious smell. Clearly it had been too long since I'd had some male company. I admit I wasn't quite the outgoing bachelorette after my ex ran off.

Fallon twitched and paused from his studies of the rubble. Then, slowly, he turned back to face me with an annoyed expression. "Did...did you say three temples?"

"Yes. Myva has—*had* four temples. One here." I pointed to the remains. "One in the North, East, and West. This is just the South Temple."

Fire erupted from his hands as he let out a snarl. I watched in fascination as the blue flames danced across his biceps, burning away the rest of his tattered shirt.

Wow!

Someone should put a warning sign on that man—Abs for days.

Also, the fire. Obviously. But he said I was safe. Not that I had any energy left to move if I wasn't.

Mr. Snarls-A-Lot threw two balls of fire at the ruined temple in frustration.

*I knew adventure was stupid. Always one more twist around the corner. However, the story of this day will make one hell of a tale to tell to Brie.*

I rested my head on the tree behind me. Fully intent on catching up on the sleep I'd been missing since Fallon showed up. Soon I felt a body slide down beside me. I peeked an eye open to see the reason for my sleeplessness settle in, his leg brushing mine.

"So," he said, putting an arm around my shoulder.

"So?" I asked warily. Snapping caimans, this man was touchy.

"I don't think you're going to like this, Rabbit." He pulled me closer, the heat of his body only making my tired mind drift closer to sleep.

"No," I whined.

"Yes," he replied, nodding.

"You said we'd be safe if I helped you with this ONE thing!"

"I said your *family* would be safe. I didn't say *you*. Or your friends. Assuming you have any. You seem like the friendly sort." He took one of my long pink braids and ran it gently around his knuckles.

"I hate you."

"Well, we'll be travel companions until the rest of the lich's hearts are destroyed." He smirked down at my withered expression. "I'll grow on ya."

"Like a plague," I muttered.

His mouth opened as his eyes widened. "Vicious little thing when tired, aren't you?"

"Sleep may be a deciding factor in future interactions, yes." With great effort, I hauled myself up and began the trek back home. "We can rest at my place before we pack up and head out." Not bothering to look back to see if I was being followed, I let the familiar path of the roads I'd traveled on my whole life lead me home.

"Oh good, I thought you would need more convincing," Fallon said, catching up to my side.

"I'm not sure what's more convincing than the threat of death."

"I could name a few."

"Please don't."

# Chapter 4

Fallon glared down at me. His large frame made an imposing figure, for sure. But this was one issue I could never
back down on. "You don't need these foolish human items,"
he said like the uncultured swine he was.

I puffed out my chest and held his glare. "You're already
dragging me on some stupid quest I have no business being on.
If you think I'm also going to spend my days eating unseasoned
slop, you may as well kill me now."

"You don't need to fill half the carriage with them! Why
are there so many?" he asked, throwing up his arms in frustration.

We'd been at this all morning. Our ideas on what packing is
were as different as night and day. The wild man in front of me
felt like a suitable weapon, and the clothes on your back were

43

a good enough choice. After informing him of my inability to heal quickly, like a demon, he conceded medicine and a few other necessities. But I guess packing a full travel carriage like a normal person was too much to ask.

Outside, my two favorite horses, Crash and Smash, neighed and fidgeted. No doubt they too grew frustrated at this heathen and his inability to grasp the concept of good food. "You already said I could take the carriage. So why do you even care what I put on it?"

"It will slow the horses down. You don't need this many spices."

My eye twitched. "I am a spice trader. I live for spices. Not to mention most of those boxes contain more cinnamon. Which need I remind you, is the only reason you'll stay sane on this journey!"

Fallon balled up his fists in frustration, but no fire engulfed his arms this time. Which was fine. I guess. If you liked men who kept their shirts on. "If they slow us down, I'm eating that one!" he said, pointing to Crash. My gray stallion huffed, but backed away from him as Fallon stormed off.

I sighed and dropped myself onto my sofa. Brie flipped the page of her romance novel from her spot on the love seat. She'd been helping me pack and watching me bicker with my new travel companion all morning. "Honestly," she began, adding more sugar to her coffee, "I think you two need to bone."

"...Have you lost your mind?"

She laughed and shrugged. "Maybe. All I'm saying is that there is some flame there and that man's looks are a gift."

Brie was right. Last night I had taken the liberty of ransacking Chili's closet for extra clothes so I could form words without the distracting presence of Fallon's chest. Sadly, the worn shirts only worsened my problem with their tight fit.

My friend sipped her coffee and smiled. "Did you see how that shirt rode up on his hips? How does one even get that V shape?"

"Down girl," I teased.

"Does he have a brother?"

I took a throw pillow from my couch and threw it at her head. She ducked just in time to let it bounce harmlessly off the wall. "You've been reading too many of those romance novels." My friend had recently restocked her never-ending supply of books. Each month, a traveling book merchant would come to town with novels written from all over the continent. As soon as he stepped foot in town, Brie would drag me with her to pick out the best books before anyone else. It kept me in a steady supply of fairy tales and fantasy novels, so I never complained. Occasionally I'd cross over into one of her romance books. As cheesy as some of them could be, they offered a beautiful escape from our predictable little village.

"Well, I'm glad you're having fun at least!" I threw one last long skirt in my chest before collapsing onto my couch. "The last thing I want is to be dragged around a death quest, even if my captor is gifted in looks."

My whole life was planned around avoiding being the chosen hero. I lay low, wore nothing too showy, and kept to myself, aside from a few friends. The thought of an epic adventure sounded great when it was in books—but that's where I wanted it to stay. In real life, those actions had terrible consequences. Even just leaving my village left one open to horrible things.

"Brie, what if I see that thing again?"

Her face became solemn as she put down her cup. She came over to my side and sat down on the couch, putting my legs in her lap. "Cinnamon, we were young. You can't keep blaming yourself for what happened."

"I know," I sighed. But the fear was still there. The bayou is a mysterious and deadly place. A few years ago, a younger, dumber me thought it would be fun to see just what mysteries lie beyond it. I paid heavily for my arrogance. The empty grave of my sister is enough of a reminder of what happens when you step out of line. The memories of a dark, crooked hand dragging Cherry underwater still haunted me. I stopped going on adventures after that. Much to my ex-boyfriend Glen's chagrin.

He had always shared my love of adventure stories and always talked about being one of Myva's chosen heroes—but losing Cherry changed things. I didn't blame him for us drifting apart, though it still hurt. We just no longer wanted the same things in life. He could push aside the terror and agony of the consequences of stepping out into the unknown. I couldn't. "Will you come with me? To the gate, at least?"

"You don't even have to ask," Brie replied.

Fallon remained in his human form and stayed away to give me time to bid farewell to my family. Naturally, Ma was sick with worry over the thought of me leaving, but I convinced her that my travel companion was strong enough to keep me safe from anything. That I would be back as soon as I could. Pa frantically restrung my bow no less than six times. Just to make sure it would fire right. After I fired arrows into any target he pointed at, Pa let out a breath of relief upon seeing that my aim was still true.

Carriage fully packed, Brie rode with me to the edge of the village outskirts where the barrier of Myva's magic used to separate us from the bayou. It disappeared once the chalice was smashed. True to Fallon's word, no demons came crashing into our area. How?—I honestly wasn't sure. He seemed too grumpy to ask.

"Everything's going to be fine," Brie said, squeezing me into a tight hug. "Just think of it as a business trip. You can sell your spices across the kingdom. Get new customers from all around."

"Yeah," I said, perking up a bit. "Of course, it's just a business trip. My brothers travel all the time, and nothing happens to them."

"There you go!" she said cheerily. "Is your demon friend going to meet up with you here soon?" Brie asked.

"Yeah, he said he'd be waiting on the main road." I turned to hoist myself up onto the front of the carriage.

"Not so fast, Hotpepper!" shouted a voice behind us.

My eyes rolled as I groaned in frustration. *Haven't I been through enough these past few days?*

"Huckabee," I growled as I turned around. Tyler Huckabee, the oldest and meanest of the five brothers, glared at me with his arms crossed over his chest. His face held a sneer only his father could love, as the much smaller Harper peeked out from behind him.

"What do you want, Tyler?" Brie asked, coming to stand at my side.

"Little girl, this has nothing to do with you," the prick said, dismissing my friend. Brie clenched her teeth in aggravation.

Tyler puffed out his chest and flexed his biceps. As if that was supposed to scare me. I knew the only reason this coward approached me now was that my brothers were nowhere in sight. No one came to the edge of the barrier unless they were leaving town. If I had to guess, this idiot followed us until we were free of any other prying eyes. Coward.

"Harper here tells me you owe him an apology," he said sternly. "Says you got drunk and chased the poor boy throughout the woods last night. So we demand compensation for his troubles!"

"That's right!" the younger brother shouted from his hiding spot.

My eyes grew wide as I placed a hand over my mouth in mock surprise. "An apology?" I gasped. "Well, of course! Just one moment, please!" Brie looked at me questioningly as I rummaged through my items on the back of the carriage.

Tyler looked at his brother in triumph and waited patiently. "Now that's more like it! It's the least you could do for scaring the poor boy," he huffed.

"Yes, yes, of course," I said in a placating tone, finding what I was looking for.

"Little women like you should mind your manners. You got no business scaring my bro—"

Tyler's face snapped back as the apple hit him square in the jaw. He stumbled back a few feet and tripped over Harper, sending them both to the ground.

Brie clutched at her sides as she laughed at the two idiots in the dirt. "Did your idiot brother tell you he tried to mug me the other night? Or did he conveniently leave that part out?" I spat at him.

The older Huckabee jumped up and balled his fists in rage. "That's just boys joking around, Cinnamon; you had no right!"

"You have a right to kiss my ass if you think I'm going to apologize for that, Huckabee!" I spat his name like a curse. "Chasing that little prick through the woods was the least I could do."

Tyler growled and stalked toward me. I pulled another apple from under my skirt and flung the fruit straight into his stomach. The force produced a satisfying grunt from the man, but he kept on his path. Tyler pushed Brie out of the way, grabbed me by the front of my frock, and slammed me against the carriage. Crash looked back and stomped his foot in frustration, but being tied to the front of the carriage meant he could do nothing but watch.

*Hissing jaguars, I'm getting so sick of men slamming me against things.*

"I'm going to give you one last chance to apologize, Cinnamon." His rancid breath rolled over my face, making me curl my lip in disgust.

"Or what?" I taunted. "You turn tail and run as soon as my brothers get here again? We all know you idiot brothers are all talk and no bite. Stomping around like you own the place when all you do is cause trouble for everybody else like a bunch of—"

The back of his hand hit me hard across the face. The sting was intense, but I refused to give him the satisfaction of crying out.

"Get off her, you pig!" Brie grabbed Tyler's arm, trying to drag him off, but he was too strong for her. Figured this prick would try his luck when he knew it was just Brie and me. If only I had some peppers to squirt in his eyes.

"Rabbit," came a cool voice.

Tyler turned to see Fallon standing a few feet behind him.

*When did he get here? The man moves like a ghost, I swear.*

The demon took in the situation with a curious look, then eyed Tyler up and down. "Is this man one of your precious friends?" Fallon asked. "He doesn't look to be a part of your family either."

"This prick? No way!" I shouted at him. A smile played on the demon's lips.

Dread poured into the pit of my stomach. "Good," he said simply.

In a flash, the oldest Huckabee was off me. I landed with a thud on my butt and looked up to see Tyler kneeling on the ground. Fallon was behind him, with a foot on his back as he held one of the man's arms. Then, with a sickening pop, Fallon twisted the captured arm back toward him. Tyler screamed in agony with another yank as fresh blood spurted from a white bone popping out of his forearm.

Brie screamed as she fell back and hurried away from the horror show in front of her. Harper gasped and stepped toward his brother.

With a cruel smirk, the demon unsheathed his sword and glanced up at the younger boy. "Get in my way, and you'll be next."

Harper stared wide-eyed for a moment. His fear got the better of him, and he stayed put.

Fallon's sword gleamed in the sunlight as he raised it above Tyler's neck.

"W-what the hell is your problem, man?!" Tyler screamed, trying to tug his broken arm free.

His cry went unanswered as his assailant positioned his sword. "Fallon, stop! What are you doing?!" I yelled.

The dark-haired man sighed heavily and looked over at me. "Isn't it obvious? I'm killing this waste of space."

"Why?!" I cried out, exasperated. It was just one thing after another with this guy.

The end of Fallon's sword plunged into Tyler's shoulder an inch or two deep. He cried out in pain but ceased to struggle. "You just said that he wasn't your friend. So he's fair game."

"He is not fair game!" I snapped. "No one here is fair game. Put down the sword, you crazy person!" My knees trembled at the feral animosity coming off the demon. He was going to do it. He'd actually kill Tyler over a slap.

The smile fell from Fallon's face. He removed the sword from Tyler's shoulder. "Don't move," he ordered. Then he walked to me and kneeled. A rough hand lifted my chin and turned my face to the side. He gazed at the reddening bruise on my cheek and frowned. "So who did this, then?"

The intensity of his dark eyes had me at a loss for words for a moment. "He did," I croaked.

"Then why are you defending him?"

"Because…because you can't just kill people!" I said. "Not over something small like this, at least."

Fallon tilted his head to the side. "Small? He hit you."

"Yeah, but you can't kill him over it!" I fully intended to get my brothers to jump him and beat him to a pulp later for sure, but not kill him.

"You absolutely can. It's effortless."

"Well...I don't want him dead over a slap. Isn't breaking his arm enough?"

Fallon said nothing. He looked back at Tyler, hunched over on the ground, clutching his arm. The demon grabbed my arm and gently helped me to my feet. "It's your village," he said sparingly. "Let's be on our way, Rabbit. I'd rather not waste any more time."

Harper seemed to find his voice then. "Wait, you can't just—"

"Harper!" I snapped. If that boy had any sense of self-preservation, he'd heed my warning. "Shut. Up."

His freckled face looked to his brother, then back to me, before closing his mouth and looking down.

*Thank goodness he's not a complete twat.*

I scrambled up to my seat in the carriage and grabbed the reins. Fallon sat next to me and placed his sword down beside him. With a gentle flick of the reins, Crash and Smash trotted through the edge of the village. I gave one last look back at my best friend to see the worry on her face. *It will be fine,* I repeated to myself like a mantra.

I just have to break a few more cups.

# Chapter 5

We traveled in silence for a while. The thought of pissing off the man next to me was more than enough incentive to keep my mouth shut. Instead of talking to him and looking at him, I took in the sights around me and planned out our route to Wandermere. The Eastern city was at least five days by carriage if what my brother told me was true—but from where I was now, the bayou felt endless.

Moss draped down from the cypress trees like a wedding veil, while the murky waters below held just enough reflection to mirror back the trees. However, it remained dark enough to keep the secrets that lay under its depths. As the horses marched down the winding path, all manner of chirping, croaking, hissing, grunting animals could be heard. Nearby, I heard a large splash of water. That was the worst.

Any form of monster could lurk nearby and use the water as a perfect cover.

*Please. Please just be an alligator!* A nasty gator was nothing new. Hell, they were even good eating. But with Volsog gate open, there was no telling what else was out there.

Beside me, Fallon made a frustrated noise and rubbed his eyes. "What is it?" he asked.

I flinched, but didn't look at him. "What is what?"

He flicked off a bit of moss that snagged on his curved horn. "You've been fidgeting and refusing to look at me since we left. What is it?" he demanded.

My mouth dropped open as I stared at him. "What is it? You nearly tore a man's arm off in front of me!" My hand waved around us to show off the scenery. "Not to mention I'm being dragged into the wilderness where literally any mythical monster could be lurking in the waters! So I guess you could say I'm a bit stressed!"

"Oh."

OH, *HE SAYS.*

"I'll be honest: I don't understand why you are upset with me for punishing that fool. He picked a fight he shouldn't have and lost. Where I come from, it would be merciful to kill something so weak. As for your fear of the myths and monsters around you: I promise you, little Rabbit, I'm the worst one. Nothing else would stand a chance of attacking us."

"Is…is that supposed to make me feel better?" I asked,

narrowing my eyes at him. "That I'm traveling with the worst of the worst?"

"Would you rather be traveling with the weakest?" he asked, glancing at me.

"I'm...No, I guess I wouldn't."

"Well, there you have it." Fallon nodded and went back to enjoying the surrounding greenery, as if that little chat solved the jaguar in the room.

"Fallon," I drawled.

"Yes?"

"You can't go around killing or maiming people." He laughed and toyed with one of my braids. The bench was enough to sit three people, but the demon seemed hell-bent on leaving me as little room as possible. I jerked my hair away and slid further to my side of the seat. "I'm serious."

My supposed protector glared at his hand where my braid used to be. As if I took away his toy. His dark eyes found mine as he mulled over my statement. I held his gaze, refusing to back down from this. Tyler was a piece of work, to be sure. But my brothers and I have traded blows with the Huckabee boys for years. He didn't deserve death for it.

A hand slid around my waist and pulled me closer to him, our faces almost touching. "Until the last phylactery is destroyed, you are mine," he growled low in his throat. "I will dispose of anyone who impedes that." Fallon held my eyes a moment longer, searching for any resistance. When he found none, he let go of my waist and backed away. "But I will refrain from killing any humans," he said, glancing back at me. "If they are smart enough to listen."

*I am a strong, independent woman.*

*I run my own segment of the renowned Hotpepper farm, and I pay my own bills.*

*I was absolutely **not** turned on by that.*

Vaguely, I wondered how good a demon's hearing was. If Fallon could hear the drum solo going on in my chest, we would have a problem.

*What is wrong with me?*

I cleared my throat and gave a slight snap to the reins, letting the horses know to speed up. "It's getting dark. We should find a place to pull off the road and camp for the night."

Soon after, I guided the horses to a clearing surrounded by tall trees, far enough away from the water's edge.

Putting some distance between Fallon and me seemed like the best course of action. I made quick work of baiting a trap and tossing it into the water for crayfish. After that, all of my focus poured into getting the horses out of their reins and setting up a small camp.

There were plenty of fallen branches and logs around, so setting up a fire seemed like a simple task. Until it came to lighting the damn thing. Fallon watched me work with a relaxed expression as I grew frustrated in my attempts to rub sticks together to catch a flame.

"Why. Won't. You. Light?!" I growled into the pile of kindling.

"Why didn't you just ask?"

I looked up to see my companion sitting across from my sad pile, chin resting on his fist as he looked at me. He brought his free hand up to his lips, made a tunnel, and shot blue flames all over the wood.

I jumped, falling on my butt as the kindling quickly took. The flames rapidly spread over the wood, solving our heat problem.

*Oh. Right. He's a demon.*

My mind drifted back to my family. More than anything, I wanted to believe Fallon meant what he said about other demons refusing to attack my village. My parents and brothers were all sitting around the dinner table, laughing and eating good food like we often did. If I couldn't be there to laugh with them, I could have at least pigged out in spirit.

It couldn't have been more than an hour or so since I had set up my trap. But the area was known to be rarely traveled; so I figured there might be an overabundance of the tasty little critters.

With a grunt, I hoisted myself up from the fire and headed over to the water. My horses trotted close behind, ready to catch a drink. Why they couldn't be bothered to come to the edge of the swamp by themselves was beyond me. They had a much better chance at kicking off a swamp ghoul than I did.

Smash shook her big black head as the cool water splashed around her hooves. The long white fur around her lower legs immediately came up as dark as the rest of her. Crash came in right behind her and barreled into the water, immediately soaking my left side. "Wow. Thanks, man."

I pulled up my sleeves and hiked my skirts higher before wading in to grab the rope. I tugged hard, but the trap barely moved. "Either we're eating good, or this sank in deep," I muttered. Smash nudged her nose into my shoulder and huffed.

"Oh, perfect, you want to help? Grab this." I presented her with the end of the rope, and she snatched it up. Then, being the best girl she is, Smash turned and walked out of the swamp bed, the trap bubbling up the surrounding water, before emerging with more crawfish than I ever expected. The catch was filled to the brim!

I let out a yell and praised Smash for her excellent work. She strutted her way back up to the campsite, flicking her tail at the other horse to rub in her new praise. I doubt her stallion cared about anything other than food, but I guess the mighty shire has her pride.

Though still bitter about my current situation, the promise of a craw boil made everything seem a bit more bearable.

Fallon, however, scrunched his nose at the sight of my glorious treasure. "What is that?" he said with disdain.

"This is crawfish, and it's about to be our dinner."

"You intend to feed me swamp spiders?" he asked, raising a brow.

"No, I intend to feed us a swamp delicacy! You do not know what blasphemy you are spouting!"

He eyed the trap again. "I don't see how such vile-looking creatures could taste good."

I looked at him with a pitying expression. "Oh, you poor, poor, sweet soul. You're gonna learn today."

My companion watched on but made no further comment as I cleaned the crawfish, threw away the nasty floaters, and brought some clean water to a rolling boil over the fire. Once the potatoes and lemons had enough time to cook, I added in the crawfish.

"Now this here is the important part, come see," I said, waving him over. The demon came to stand beside me and peered into the pot obediently. "Most people think you can just add in the seasonings, fixins, and craw right away with the rest of the boil. Those people are wrong, and that's why we have to eat before showing up to their parties, cause the damn shellfish never peel right!"

"Well, that is just wildly unacceptable," he replied dryly.

"I'm going to ignore that sarcasm. Anyway, there are levels to this! Once the potatoes are al dente, then you can add the crawfish. Stir them up for no more than a few minutes, then lower the flame."

Fallon flicked his wrist, and the campfire seemed to simmer down.

I blinked in surprise as the water lost some of its boil. "My, my, you are a nifty one." I walked back to the cart to grab my seasonings and corn. "Now you can add the good stuff!" With a flourish, I dumped the rest of the boil into the pot. Immediately I was rewarded with the mouthwatering smell of a promised feast.

Placing two mugs on a nearby stump, I pulled out a bottle of mead from my pocket and filled them up.

I could feel Fallon's burning gaze on me without even looking at him. "Hold on," he said, pointing to the bottle. "Did you just pull an entire bottle of liquor out of your skirt?"

"Yes."

He looked down at my ankle-length blue skirt as if it held the secrets of the world. "I don't even see pockets."

"Oh, they're on the inside of the outer skirt." I pulled back the top blue skirt to show the white one underneath and pulled a loaf of bread and dried beef from the large side pocket. Thankfully, Crash only got my left side wet where I kept the mead. "I always keep extra snacks in here."

If I thought his face was beautiful before, it was downright unholy when he laughed. Fireflies danced around us, illuminating his strong features in the dim light. If I hadn't seen his brutality firsthand earlier in the day, I might have mistaken this moment as something romantic. The smell of the crawfish cooking over an open fire, the moon shining over the moss-covered canopy as its light glittered green jewels on the water's surface. My hand twitched with the desire to reach out and touch the ink hair falling across his face.

*Pull yourself together!*

Instead, I handed him his mug. "The food should be done now. I'll fix you a plate."

He chuckled and took the offered mug. "Right, your swamp spiders. I admit I'm excited to try more of your human dishes. It smells remarkable."

Try as I might, I couldn't stop the swell of pride from forming in my chest.

*This man and his damn food compliments.*

With both our plates piled high, I broke off one of the crawfish's heads from its body and showed him the proper way to slurp it down.

He frowned at it for a moment before following suit. I watched, transfixed, as Fallon closed his eyes and...groaned.

Heat pooled in my lower belly as my gaze locked on to a trail of juice that slid down the side of his full lips. Absently, he licked it away, along with most of my sanity.

Quickly averting my gaze, I stuffed a potato in my mouth and kept eating. The demon tore into the food like he'd never eaten a day in his life. Before I could even finish my first plate, he piled on seconds, then downed his mug.

He eyed the mug for a moment, then reached for the bottle

to pour another round. "What is this ale? Where has it been all my life?"

"It's blackberry mead," I said.

At his confused look, I continued. "Honey wine."

Nodding in approval, he continued to eat. And eat. And eat. I guess I shouldn't have been too surprised. The man had to be at least seven feet tall, not counting the horns. I think that meant no leftovers for breakfast.

Soon after I ate my fill, I set up a few blankets to settle into bed.

Sadly, no matter how much I tossed and turned, sleep did not come. The sounds of the bayou made my imagination race with all the terrible possibilities of what could happen while I slept. Every time I closed my eyes, another hiss or another snarl would cause me to snap up again.

"I told you," Fallon said from his spot, resting on a tree. "Whatever is in this forest is no match for me. Go to sleep."

I turned to my side and glared at him across the waning campfire. "That doesn't make it any less scary! I still don't fully trust you either."

A laugh rumbled deep in his chest. "If I kill you, who will cook me more swamp spiders?"

"Oh, you are just hilarious," I said, voice full of disdain, then turned over again, trying to catch at least a few hours of sleep.

"What was that?!" Fallon shouted with a gasp.

I popped up again, heart racing. "What? What did you hear!"

The demon looked around, covering his mouth with his hand. "Ah! The wind!"

"You are just the worst today!" I snapped back at him before lying down. "Wondering why I can't trust you when you're over here acting like a downright scoundrel. No." I paused, turning back to him. "Scoundrel is too innocent of a word. You, sir, are a rapscallion!" Fallon put a hand on his chest and gasped as if utterly scandalized before his shoulders shook with the effort not to laugh. With an irritated huff, I dug my head into my pillow and tried again for sleep.

Fallon's body snapped up in alert. "Rabbit, look out!"

I jumped up with a scream, blankets wrapped around my ankles, and hopped towards the spot where my guardian rested against a tree. My breath shook as I looked around frantically and dove behind him. "What was it?!"

Fallon burst into laughter and patted my shoulder. "I'm sorry, I couldn't resist."

My pillow met his face with a soft thud, but I didn't move from my place beside him. If there were monsters that would attack in the night, they could eat his ass first. "I'm going to sleep now," I snarled, trying not to think of the fact that I was practically snuggled up to his waist. Fear eclipsed pride, I guess.

"Good night," he replied with a smug smile.

Before drifting off to sleep, I felt the barest touch of Fallon's hand resting on my side.

The journey through the rest of the bayou became a blur of weariness, more unidentifiable noises, and horribly muggy weather. After the first two days, we managed to fall into a routine. The day was spent making idle chatter as the horses plodded on. Occasionally I'd show Fallon something about the landscape or whatever creature caught his fancy. By his own admission, his homeland was a frozen mountain where very few things lived. The variety of life, as well as the hot weather, were utterly foreign to him.

At night we'd set up camp, and I'd cook up whatever creature he killed. For someone who griped so heavily on my packing the proper amount of spices, he sure went through a lot of them in his quest to devour every type of food the land offered. I could only imagine how dull the cuisine on his mountain must have been.

On the fourth night, I found myself giddy to be reaching the end of the bayou. I'd never actually been that far from home. Or anywhere else, really.

"Did you pass through Wandermere on your way to my village?" I asked him as we settled in for the night.

"No," Fallon said lazily, tucking himself into one of my blankets. "Once the spell took over, my mind was about as useless as a slug. The first memory I have is you hitting me with that cinnamon branch."

"Ah yes. Good times."

The demon stared hard into the flames of the campfire. "These woods do remind me of something, though."

"Oh, what's that?" Curiosity burned as I took my place on the opposite side of the fire. I spread out my bottom blanket before snuggling into the top one. Aside from telling me about the landscape of his home, Fallon talked little about it.

His voice was grave as he spoke. "Rabbit, have you ever heard of the Hungry Man?"

I narrowed my eyes on him. "Is this your way of telling me you need a snack?"

He shook his head with a wry smile. "No. Never mind, it's foolish. Just an old wives' tale." The raven-haired man scanned the dark outlines of the surrounding trees. His mouth formed a thin line.

*Cin, he's just trying to scare you. Don't ask. Just go to sleep. Don't ask!* "About what?" *Dammit.*

Not taking his eyes off the shadows of the night, Fallon shifted upright.

"Well, it's said that when a man gets lost in the woods and starves, he becomes a ghoul known as a Hungry Man."

I huffed and settled back down. "That doesn't seem so scary."

The demon's dark eyes found mine. "You wouldn't think so. But once a spirit becomes a Hungry Man, they can no longer discriminate between food and, well…people. They use the shadows of the night to grab anything they can and rend the flesh from its bones. But no matter how much they eat, they can never be full."

Despite my best efforts not to, I chanced a glance at the darkness beyond the fire. "But you can fight one, right? You said you were the worst of the worst."

"Oh, of course," Fallon said, warming his hands by the fire.

I relaxed a little.

"If I can catch him in time. His shadow hands are said to be as fast as lightning. You never know when he could reach out and grab you."

Movement caught my eye. My vision snapped left to find a shadowed hand creeping close to my foot. I shrieked in fear. Heart pounding in my ears, I bounded around the fire and dove onto Fallon for protection. "I SAW THE HAND!" My body shook as I pointed across to where I had just been lying. "KILL IT, KILL IT!"

Fallon's chest shook. I looked up at him to see him grinning ridiculously. He held up his hand and wagged his fingers, their shadows dancing across the fire.

My face burned. "You…are terrible."

His arms came around my torso, settling me into his lap as he laughed. "You make it so easy."

I swatted his hands away as I clambered off him. As I stomped back to my original spot, a screech sounded off in the distance, making me freeze. Glancing around, I tugged my blanket tighter around my shoulders. "There is no such thing as a Hungry Man."

Fallon lay down, tucking himself in again. "Or is there?"

My skin prickled at another unidentifiable sound. "It's probably just an owl!"

"Mm-hmm."

Growling in frustration, I stomped back to Fallon and lay down next to him. I could feel the grin on his face without even turning around. "It's just so you get eaten first," I snapped, burrowing into my blankets.

It was still dark when I woke up again. Cold fog rolled over me like a wet sheet, causing me to burrow further into my blankets. Then, far into the darkness, I heard the faint sound of soft crying.

That...couldn't be Fallon, right? I couldn't picture the demon with any other emotion than rage or smugness. I tried to get up, but my body felt too heavy. Sleep clouded my mind as the crying grew louder. My hand reached beside me to see if he was still there, but I felt nothing but the cold ground. Finally, I groaned and forced myself to sit up.

"Fallon?" There was no answer. The fog was so thick I could barely see my nose in front of my face. *I know I fell asleep next to him.* "Where did he go?" My head felt like it was made of stone.

Through the fog, the crying voice seemed to speak:

"—nimon…" The rest of it was lost to the night air. I tried to focus on it to see which direction it was coming from. It was so hard to even think. Rubbing my eyes did little to dispel the lethargy, but I shook off as much as I could.

"Fallon, is that you?" I called out.

"Cin." The voice was soft and sounded scared. It rang sharply in my head like I was supposed to know it.

I got to my feet to try and get closer. "I'm here! Where are you?"

"…I'm………here." Goddess, that voice sounded so familiar. "…Sister……I'm here."

Horror flooded my body and my knees buckled. Cherry. That was Cherry's voice! My hands shook as I frantically looked around the fog for her. If she was alive…if Cherry somehow survived, I had to find her!

"Cherry!" I screamed. "Just keep talking. I'm coming!" I scrambled to my feet and ran toward the voice.

"…I'm here…"

Mud squelched under my bare feet as I tore through the foliage. It was so cold. I'd never known that Kinnamo could get this cold. If Cherry was in the water, then she could freeze. I had to get to her. "Keep talking!" I begged. My words came out as a mist around my face. Was that normal? How could you see your breath?

My foot caught on a vine, and I tripped, crashing into a slope and rolling down into the water. I shivered as my hands sank into the mud of the bank, but I pushed myself back up. "Cherry?"

"I'm here."

I turned to see a figure standing further into the water. It raised a hand to me, calling me closer. "I'm here."

Tears spilled down my face as I got close enough to make out the sweet face of my little sister. Matted black braids clung to her face, giving contrast to her precious dark brown skin. She was covered in dirt and muck, but it was her! She was alive! Cherry smiled at me and called me closer. "I'm cold. It's so cold here."

"It's OK, I've got you now. I've got blankets at my camp. We can warm up and go home!" The water rose to my waist as I waded in further. *How long has she been here? Her legs must be frozen.*

"Rabbit, stop!"

Behind me, Fallon stood looking positively frantic on the bank. His hair was a mess around his face, and his clothes seemed rumpled as if he'd just forced them on. Odd. I didn't know the demon could look so disheveled.

"Well, don't just stand there. Help me get my sister out of this water." I turned back to Cherry to see her eyeing the demon with an unreadable expression. It was only natural to be scared, I suppose. "Don't worry," I said, reaching for her. "He looks terrifying, I know. But he's with me."

"Dammit, woman, that's not your sister, stop!" He took a

step into the water and grasped the hilt of his sword. "Back away slowly and come to me. Now." The warning in his tone felt half like a threat. As if I was a child in need of reprimand.

My face scrunched up at him in indignation. "Did you eat some mushrooms you found on the ground or something? I don't know where else you'd get that tone from. Just help me get her out of here." I smiled sheepishly at Cherry and opened my mouth to apologize for his rude behavior.

"Rabbit!" he roared. "Look behind her!"

"What?" Cherry took her gaze off Fallon finally to smile up at me. She raised her arms to me again, waiting for me to pull her to me. But I leaned to the side, past her face, and looked down. There, peeking up over the edge of the water, was the most hideous black dog I'd ever seen. Its maw held sharp dagger-like fangs and long fur ran down from the top of its head. The fur spiked like needles as it rose further out of the water. I followed the trail of spiked fur down its back to the base of its tail, which curved up and...ended in Cherry's back.

I stumbled back away from her. My sister's body suddenly shimmered and vanished as a raccoon-like hand shot out from where she stood and grabbed my shoulder. The black dog dove underwater, dragging me with it by its freakish tail-hand. I tried to scream, but my lungs filled with water. Desperately I tried clawing the hand off my shoulder and kicked at the beast. Its needle-fur dug into my calves, but I kept kicking and thrashing.

The creature paid no mind to my protests as it dragged me deeper down. *This must be what happened four years ago,* I thought. *This thing took my only sister from me. Now it has me too.*

My ma's face entered my mind. She was going to have to put flowers on another empty grave. I remembered how quickly she wasted away, how she cried every night. It took months to get her out of her despair, and I was about to do it to her all over again.

*I'm sorry, Ma. I'm so sorry.*

A lack of air burned in my chest as I gave a few more feeble kicks. In an instant, the pressure released from my shoulder. The surrounding water turned dark red as the dog screeched and thrashed. I broke free and desperately swam toward the surface, coughing up water.

I looked over to see the dog impaled on Fallon's sword; it continued to bite and snap at him. The demon grabbed the beast by the ends of its jaw and pulled them apart. The dog made a sickening screech as its jaws snapped before it died and sank into the water—not that I had an ounce of sympathy for the wretched thing.

With the grace of a half-dead fish, I swam toward the edge of the water before collapsing on the bank. My arms and legs felt like pudding beneath me. Twigs and mud clung to my body and my now-ruined braids. I never wanted to move again. *Fresh hell, that was awful.*

In a blur, Fallon stood beside me. *Just how fast can that man move?* Maybe I was just too tired to notice his approach. Despite killing the creepy dog, he looked no worse for wear. His clothes were muddy, and there was blood spatter on his shirt—but I'd bet money none of it was his.

"Fancy seeing you here." I grinned, trying to lighten the mood. *Stupid, what was that?*

He grimaced and knelt. "Are you hurt anywhere?" Then, without waiting for an answer, he began checking over my body for any injuries.

I looked away from him. The last thing I wanted to see was the pity in his eyes. I should have known better. "Oh, I'm just peachy. Never better."

Fallon hooked an arm around my torso and another around my legs and picked me up. I gave a surprised squawk as he settled me against his chest and began walking up to the bank. "What are you doing?"

The demon spoke in a soft tone one would reserve for comforting a wounded animal. "I'm carrying you back to the campsite. After that, we're going to wash you off and put you to rest." His gaze never left the path in front of him. Quickly, Fallon made his way through the forest and back to our latest resting spot. The horses slept next to the carriage without a care in the world. Our fire still held tiny embers that sent out sparks to compete with the night stars.

"I can walk on my own," I hissed at him. My throat felt tight as I fought away tears. *So stupid.* I needed to get away from him before I made an even bigger fool of myself.

"I know you can. But you're half frozen, you saw something terrible and upsetting, and you need to rest. So let me help you."

He set me down next to the river bank with a gentleness I never expected from someone so terrifying. It wasn't until he let go that I truly realized how cold I was. My hands shook in front of me, and all I wanted to do was curl up and rekindle the fire. Fallon removed a small braid from the front of my face and plucked a twig from another. He sighed as he sat down behind me and began to unravel one of them.

I jerked my head away and shot him a glare. "What do you think you're doing? Those took forever!"

Something like pity floated across his face as he took in my shivering form. "Yes, and they were stunning, but now they are covered in swamp mess, and I doubt you'll be able to wash all of it out with them still in place."

He began on the left side of my scalp, quickly un-fashioning each braid. Fallon's hands were lean and elegant for a man. His fingers combed through each segment, freeing the tight curls from each other before moving to the next braid. I closed my eyes at the soothing sensation. He was right about everything, as much as I hated to admit it. It took everything I had not to just collapse against him in exhaustion.

Tears I'd been fighting back rebelled in my eyes. I swallowed hard as the shame built in the pit of my stomach. "I'm sorry." The whisper was all I could manage without turning into a blubbering fool.

Fallon ran his hands through a new section of free hair. "That was a water dog. They hunt by luring their prey into the water, as you saw. Their magic can even make you see things you can't resist."

"I should have known better."

He paused his movements. "How? Do you have a background in fighting monsters I should know about?" he said with a grin. "I've seen creatures far bigger than you fall victim even to lesser magic." His hands started up again, undoing the last of the tight braids.

My shoulders shook as the floodgates opened. Hot tears spilled down my face as I frantically tried to wipe them off.

"My little sister disappeared four years ago," I choked out. "Brie, Chili, and I had gone into the bayou to explore, as stupid kids do. Despite being the youngest, Cherry, being the bravest, ran further ahead than us. But that black...water dog snatched her and pulled her into the river. We searched for weeks, but she was nowhere. It took my sister, and I fell for the damn thing again!"

Fallon stopped my movements and put his hand on my forehead, forcing me to lean back against him. His arms came around my waist and held me tight. His back was so warm. He rested his chin on the top of my head and slowly stroked his thumb on my arm. "Just cry," he breathed.

I did. I sobbed against him until my eyes were red and puffy. My hands grasped the arms around my waist as I held on to him. All the while, he sat patiently, just holding me.

When the tears finally stopped, Fallon made his way over to the carriage to grab the soap, a knife, and a hair cleanser at my request. He returned and untied the laces of my boots. Slipping each one off before starting on the fastenings on the side of my skirt. His fingers rushed along the garment, and I stiffened as he began to tug it off. At my hesitation, he stilled and raised an eyebrow.

"Contrary to whatever stories of demons and monsters you've been told, the sight of a quivering, crying woman does nothing for my arousal. You are safe from me tonight."

"Tonight?" I asked.

Fallon gave a wry smile and winked. "I said I might grow on you."

A laugh escaped my throat as I shoved him away and got up. Any point of decency seemed like a moot point after crying all over him. So I stripped myself of the rest of my clothing and headed into the river with the jar of soap and knife. After today, I doubt I'd ever step into water unarmed again.

It wasn't the first time I'd been naked in front of a man, but I could feel my cheeks grow hot as I dunked my head in the water. If he wasn't going to make a big deal of it, then neither was I. At the very least, the water was warm. Whatever cold spell that magic dog caused must have faded away when it died. My cold limbs tingled at the warm sensation as I sank in further. I held the knife in my mouth as the lavender soap soothed my fried senses. Then, scooping some on my hands, I scrubbed off the muck of the day.

I squeaked in surprise as the soap was taken from my hand. Fallon snorted in amusement as he took some for himself. "What? I'm filthy too."

My jaw hung open at the sight of a very naked demon standing beside me. I mean, I was naked too. I just didn't think he'd be getting in with me.

My companion turned his back to me and began washing himself. The tight muscles on his back rippled with movement. And good lord, I needed to turn around. That was so rude. I shook my head and spun around. Deftly, I scrubbed the rest of the mud off before realizing I left the hair cleanser on the bank.

"Did you need this?" Fallon asked, holding out the jar of hair cleaner. I swallowed thickly and took it, nodding. "It smells like fruit. What is it?"

I put a small bit of it in my hands and began running it through my hair. The curly locks reached below my shoulder blades now that the water weighed them down. "It's a smrfm mrrm—"

"The knife, woman."

*Oh right.* After taking the weapon out of my mouth, I tried again. "It's a special hair cleaner the women in my village make. It's to keep it healthy, so it doesn't frizz up in our humid weather."

Fallon shifted closer to me. The heat of his body was a whisper away from brushing up against mine. Thick strands of his raven hair brushed up against my shoulder as he leaned in closer and inhaled. "I imagine the women in this realm must be willing to pay a hefty price to make their scent so alluring."

It would have been really useful if my mouth could make the words to answer him. However, my tongue seemed to swell into a useless mess. Fallon ran a hand through my soap-covered hair as my heart set off on a solo stampede. His free hand reached down to take more of the cleaner before working it into my curls. Fallon's easy ministrations caused my head to loll back slightly, allowing him easier access.

I couldn't tell if I was relaxed or aroused. Both? The situation as a whole was ridiculous. No less than three days into the journey, and I was tits out in the bayou with the man who threatened my home.

Fallon's hand slid up the nape of my neck before gliding down the length of my hair, igniting goosebumps down my spine. Oh goddess, that felt nice. I mean, did he really do anything that bad? Sure Tyler got his arm broken, but the man is objectively terrible. On the other hand, Fallon did just save me and kill the monster that took my sister.

Strong hands came up the side of my head as his fingers massaged the mixture into my hair. My teeth clenched to fight back a moan. The effect this man had on me was like nothing I'd felt before. With my ex-boyfriend, Glen, there had been clumsy fumbling and awkward kisses. Both of us were too young and inexperienced to know what we were doing. But judging by the way this demon simply touched my head, the thought of him going any lower was almost too much to bear.

Tyler could get by on one arm for a while. Peaceful contentment drew a sigh from my lips as I leaned in closer to his touch. Or maybe I was just too tired and horny to think straight about what I was doing. With no small effort, I forced my eyes to flutter open and come back from the hypnotic sensation of Fallon's fingers. In front of us, I noticed a moss-covered log drifting slowly by. Or rather, toward us.

"Fallon?" I whispered softly.

"Yes?"

"There is one more bayou delicacy that you haven't tasted yet."

Interest piqued, he removed his hands from my mane and regarded me with questions in his eyes. "What would that be?"

The loss of his touch was a crime, but it brought me back to reality. The log in front of me was nearly a meter away, so I stepped forward and swung my knife as hard as I could to where I guessed the snout would be. A symphony of teeth hissed in protest as the alligator reared back and turned its giant head. Wasting no time, I took the dagger and drove it in between the head and the creature's back, severing its spine. The gator's massive body twitched and spasmed before it went still. Water splashed high in the air as its bonecrushing tail slammed once more into the waves.

Before it could sink to the bottom, I grabbed the alligator by its neck and began guiding it to the shore. Alligators had a nasty habit of making their way into Boohail. It wasn't often that you'd find them in the river flowing through town, but when you did, it was always somehow when someone was bathing or when children played in the water. You never could be too careful. At the very least, they were delicious after you fried them up.

"Could you give me a hand with this?" Turning back, I saw my demon standing there with an astonished expression on his face.

Hands still full of soapy hair cleanser, he looked to the gator, then back at me, then back to the gator. A frown insinuated itself between his dark brows. "That man who hit you back at the village. Was he your lover?"

Startled, my hands slipped from the gator's neck. The creature's body splashed into the water before sinking to my feet. "Tyler?!" I croaked out. "Ew, no."

He took a step forward before bending over to wipe the

soap from his hands. "The younger one then?" he asked succinctly.

"Also no, I don't have one." Wrapping my arms back around my catch, I began dragging the gator to shore once more. "Even if I did, it would never be a Huckabee." The mere thought was laughable at best.

"Excellent, that makes this easy." Fallon strode toward me with confidence no naked man should have. Even one as painfully stunning as the otherworldly beauty before me. His smoothly muscled arm glistened as water droplets rolled off him. The broad plains of his chest leading down to his ripped abdomen were so perfect you'd think they were carved from priceless marble and smoothed to a fine finish. As he approached the bank, his body rose higher out of the water until I found myself staring at what would only be considered as another weapon.

"Hot damn." *OH MY FILÉ POWDER, I SAID THAT OUT LOUD!* Scarlet embarrassment raced across my dark skin as I tried to look anywhere but at Fallon's dick.

The splashing of water alerted me to his approach. He removed the gator from my hands and effortlessly threw it out of the water. The beast landed with a solid thud near the campfire.

Fallon cupped my chin when I refused to look at him. "You certainly know how to feed a man's ego, Rabbit." His coal eyes took me in with a downright predatory expression as a crooked smile tugged at the corner of his mouth. "I don't think I'll be letting you go after we finish this quest."

Fireflies danced a lively jig in the pit of my stomach. "W-what do you m-mean?" The question came out with a stammer as his free hand traced my collarbone and up my neck.

A devilish grin sent shock waves straight to my core.

"I mean, I'm going to take you as my wife when this is all over."

"That wasn't part of the deal, demon!" I imagine my retort would have sounded a lot stronger if it hadn't come out so desperately.

"Then you shouldn't have been so horribly interesting." The heat of Fallon's breath danced across my cheek as his hand buried itself in my hair. Lips gently brushed across my ear as he spoke. "Finish washing, love. I'll help fix your hair after."

With that, he placed a kiss on my cheek and strode off to the campsite. Losing his warmth nearly took me off my feet and left an emptiness I didn't expect. I stood there at the edge of the water for a moment, stunned.

*What... what the fuck was that?*

# Chapter 6

Things were weird the following day. Fallon seemed to be in an unusually good mood as we packed up camp and headed for Wandermere. He even stopped to pet the horses and called them by their names instead of the usual "Hoof Beast."

The demon glanced over when he noticed me staring. He tore off a piece of the gator jerky he'd been eating and offered it to me. I took it and turned back to the road ahead.

"So, are we going to talk about what you said last night?"

"What's to discuss, my love?"

I flinched at the casual promotion from Rabbit to Love. "That! Right there, what is that about?"

Fallon leaned closer and draped an arm around my shoulders. "Do humans in your culture not use pet names?" He furrowed his brows and thought for a moment. "I could say 'Honey,' but it doesn't quite fit."

"You shouldn't be calling me either! My name is Cinnamon. Or Cin for short. I'm not your wife either."

"Well, of course not, love. I'd need to put my mark on you for that." He brushed my curly hair away from my neck and traced it softly. "I'd give you a bite right here and transfer some of my magic into you."

A slight shock of electricity went through me as he kissed my shoulder just above the collarbone. I jumped and pushed him away. Scooting as far away as the seat allowed, I shot him a dark glare.

Fallon laughed and settled back into place. "Of course, that would trigger the honeymoon phase, and we wouldn't be able to keep our hands off each other. As tempting as you are, love, I'd rather not fuck you senseless in a deadly forest."

"I'm sorry, honeymoon phase? What is that?"

His lips quirked. "The transfer of magic between a mated pair of my kind acts as an aphrodisiac. It lasts for a few weeks on average."

My mind spun with that new information. Weeks of uncontrollable lust? These demons really didn't play around. "I have agreed to absolutely none of that!"

"Why not? You mentioned you were unattached, we've gotten along quite well, the attraction is there, and I'm clearly strong enough to protect you."

He was, without a shadow of a doubt, the most arrogant man I'd ever met. "You've known me for four days!"

Fallon grinned and took the reins from my hands and flicked them to have the horses pick up the pace. "Yes. And in those four days, I've met your parents—"

"You threatened my parents."

"Semantics. We've saved each other multiple times, been naked together, and I saw you kill a giant lizard with zero hesitation." He reached over to snag me around the waist and pulled me to him. "That last one sealed the deal for me, to be honest. I've always wanted a fierce mate."

"That's it? The basis for demon marriage is killing an alligator?" I frowned up at him but didn't bother to pull away.

His grip around me tightened as we came up to a long bridge. His coal eyes narrowed as he scanned the area. The wilds of the bayou seemed to stop at its edge. It sat atop a large river with a sea of grasslands on the other side. To the east, I could make out a whisper of a city outline. "It certainly helps."

Four burly men jumped out in front of the horses, causing them to rear up and stop. One man, I assume the leader, stepped up to grab Smash by her rein and pull her still. His hair was all but gone, except for a ring of scraggly hair going from his ears to the back of his head. I don't know why balding men choose to keep that. Just shave it off.

He squinted his eyes as he looked me over, ignoring my companion and the increasingly irritated horse at the end of his hand.

"Well, well, what's a pretty thing like you do—OOORFF!"

An enraged Smash stole the breath from his lungs, bringing her knee up to his family jewels. He heaved over, gasping, which was still too close for the mare's liking. She reared up and smashed her hoof on the man's shoulder before kicking him again for good measure. The leader fell face-first into the dirt, out cold. The three remaining men looked at their fallen comrade with wide eyes.

I couldn't help it. Laughter burst out of me before I could stop it. Fallon joined in, and soon we were both a hot mess, laughing at the wannabe bandit on the ground.

This seemed to anger his friends as another stepped forward with a knife out. However, he was smart enough to stay out of reach from the ornery mare.

"Let's see how much you bastards want to laugh when you're carved up on the street with your valuables taken!" His thin face scrunched up in a sneer. "Or maybe we'll just take turns with that pretty whore of yours as payment."

His remaining cohorts laughed in agreement, as if my horse didn't just take out their leader.

*Oh. Bandit rapists. How cliché.* I couldn't even pretend to be surprised. Every adventure book I've ever read had at least one scene where the hero dashingly defeats a group of bandits to save the honor of a fair maiden. Only I wasn't traveling with a hero. No. I was the lucky sucker saddled with a villain. I looked over at Fallon to find the man missing.

A scream from the thin-faced man drew my attention back to him. My villain had the stupid sap pinned to the ground and was punching him repeatedly in the head. Blood spurted from the man's face as a tooth flew away from Fallon's flaming fists.

*There goes another shirt.*

"Holy shit, that man's a demon!" one of the other men cried.

*Did he just realize that? The horns didn't give it away? Not the brightest lot.*

"Quit your bellyaching and get him! He's killing Jeff!"

The last of the four was a stout man with red hair. He wore the tattered clothes of a field hand and held a spear. The bellyacher in question held his knife and eyed the demon with uncertainty, but took a step forward.

As much as I trusted Fallon to fight off the occasional bandit, three at once was a bit much. I jumped into the back of the cart and grabbed my bow and quiver. It had been a while since I'd really used the thing, but Pa demanded all his children know the basics of shooting in case we ever needed it. If I survived this adventure, I'd have to let him get in his "I told you so." The old man has earned that much.

Grabbing an arrow from the quiver, I lined it up at the spearman. Fallon would have the most trouble fighting against a long-range weapon in a hand-to-hand situation.

The demon snarled in anger before grabbing the punching bag named Jeff by the ankles and swinging him into the other man with the knife.

89

The knifewielder went flying and slammed into the bridge's handrail before skittering over the wood planks and coming to a stop.

"GARY!" the spearman shouted as he looked back at the fallen man on the bridge. He clutched his spear tight and aimed at Fallon, who was still holding the unconscious Jeff by the ankle. "You'll pay for that!"

I rolled my eyes. "I mean, not what I would say to the man who just beat your friend with your other friend like he was a ragdoll. But live your best life, I guess."

The spearman glanced back at him as his face swelled red with rage. "I'm not scared of a filthy demon and his whore!" He grinned and turned his spear at me. "After I finish with him, I'll have you on your knees!" He licked his gross lips in a lewd display, which was really all the invitation I needed.

I pulled back the arrow and let it fly. It sunk into the right side of his chest, and he stumbled several steps back. Fallon whipped Jeff around again, slamming the spearman into the air, where he fell into the river with a scream. The current quickly took him underwater before spitting him out over the waterfall a few yards down.

*Man, that's a fast current.*

My demon growled in frustration and threw Jeff to the side of the road. "DAMMIT!" he snarled.

"What's up with you? You won."

His shoulders sank as he looked up at me. "I hit him off the river. Most likely killing him."

"Yeah, I don't think he's getting back up after that." I wasn't sure if the other men were ever getting up again either, for that matter.

"I gave you my word I would try not to kill any more of your precious humans." Fallon scowled at the mess of men around him. The flames had dissipated from his arms, with the remnants of the shirt smoking slightly.

*Is he...ashamed?* He took what I said to heart. Maybe I wasn't traveling with a straight villain. Perhaps he was just villain-adjacent. I could work with that.

"Fallon, it's fine," I told him in a soft tone. Shrugging the quiver off my shoulder, I placed the bow and arrows back in the cart. "I hold no love for rapists and thieves. If you didn't kill them, I'm sure they would have done worse to me. Hence why I shot the last one. Hell, I think Smash killed the leader."

His head rose to look me in the eye. "You are not upset?"

"No. They were rapists. Please kill rapists."

The demon grinned a wicked smile, and I sent a curse down to my lady bits for getting a little too excited.

"This I can do."

"That's the spirit," I said, patting the seat next to me. He jumped up and sat next to me, flicking the reins. The horses started up again and trotted across the bridge. On the horizon, I could see the outline of the next city. Cup number two was close at hand.

Fallon put an arm back around my shoulders, settling my

91

head against his chest. "Does this mean you've agreed to be my wife?"

"No, you're still a rapscallion."

He scoffed and gave me a teasing grin. "I've earned at least a few points for dispatching those bandits."

"Is my hand in marriage a point-based system? Are we going to joust to see who gets to decide where to hold the wedding reception?" I asked sarcastically.

"What better way to prove myself? How about we make a bet." Fallon rubbed his chin thoughtfully. "If I can rack up enough points to win you by the end of our task, you agree to be mine. How many points would I need to win your heart?"

"One thousand," I said instantly.

He balked and eyed me like I was a crazy woman. "You're a stingy one." Honestly, it just seemed like an impossible number, so I went for it.

Marriage to a demon was nowhere in my life's plan, right up there with never going on a stupid adventure that could get me killed. But Fallon was the pushy type. Better to play along than anger a man who could beat up another man with... another man. "That's my price. Take it or leave it."

"One thousand points," he grit out. "What are your other terms?"

I blinked, unsure of what else to ask for. "I think that's it. If you can make me happy or do something good, I'll give you points. If you can't reach one thousand, I will go home safe and sound after the last cup is destroyed."

"So it's a deal then?" The demon held out his hand to shake on it.

In the corners of my memory, I could hear my grandma telling me that only fools make deals with demons, as that is how the King of Death buys souls. She was also a crazy old bat who talked to ravens, so maybe the insurance of Fallon's interest was worth it. He may have needed me to smash the fake goddess' cups, but so could any other human. If he were to get bored with me and replace or kill me, I didn't think there'd be much I could do to stop him. When the quest was over, I'd have the option to find an excuse to deny him the total points and escape.

"Deal." I took his hand and gave it a firm shake.

His grip on my hand tightened as his predatory grin shot thrills down my spine. Alarm jolted through me, but before I could withdraw, he pulled me to straddle his lap.

Once he caught me, Fallon pressed his parted lips against mine. My breath snagged. I felt a rush of helplessness, a sinking surrender to the warmth that left me weak in the knees. My reservations blurred as my mind drowned to nothingness. He ran a hand slowly up the back of my neck before fisting it through my pink locks, trapping me in place. He tilted my head and kissed me gently at first and then with a fierce intensity that forced me to cling to him as the world spun and burned away. His demanding tongue parted my lips, tasting me until my nerves fried at the wild sensations I didn't know I was capable of feeling. I cried out as he yanked my head back.

I felt the electrifying touch of his tongue against my neck. His breath against the soft flesh felt like wildfire in my veins.

His whisper seemed to eat away at my core. "You think I can't see right through your little game, my love?" Fallon trailed his hand under my skirt, pushed my snack pocket aside, and gently caressed my thigh before grabbing my ass and grinding me to him. "Deny me as much as you want, but we both know how this will end. In the meantime, I'll enjoy breaking down those defenses you've put up. I wonder if you'll still be counting points after I've shredded your clothes with my teeth. Then, after you've been pinned to the ground, my hands teasing those large breasts of yours as I kiss them, lick them…until the tips grow hard under my tongue, then I would trace my fangs over them so gently…"

My mind tried to signal my hands to push him away, to stop this before I lost the bet before it had barely begun, but all I did was hold him tighter as he ran his tongue against my neck.

"…I'll kiss my way down your body as I find all the little places that make you moan before I settle in between these thick thighs."

His free hand went back, caressing my thighs before moving up my ass and down again. He groaned deep in his throat and gently bit my neck. "Do you know how hard it was not to bury my head in between them as we bathed together? You may call me a demon, little Rabbit, but you're the cruel party here. Taunting me with that sweet cunt just out of reach." I shuddered as his fingers dipped into my inner thigh, a whisper away from my core.

"How many points will you give me when I taste your cunt? I'll lick my way through it, slowly, getting deeper and deeper until I've found the little jewel of your clit...and I would circle my tongue on it until I feel it swell. I'll lick it, stroke it... until you squeezed these thighs around my head, until you've grabbed me by the horns and guided me deeper into you. I'll suck on you then. But not enough to give you a reprieve. I want you begging, you see. I'll do it so gently...so delicately... that you stop being so fucking careful with me and show me that fiery hellion I know you've been hiding. Then I would put my tongue inside you...taste you...eat you...as I rub your clit. I won't stop until you're shaking, screaming for me to take you. I'll see just how much I can torment you until you open up for me. That's where my gentleness stops. I'll come inside you and take you roughly. I'll make you take every last bit of me until I'm burned in your memory. That's just how you like it, isn't it, love? You can keep up the lie of the docile little lamb for your false goddess, but never from me."

I cried out as his thumb slid my panties over to brush against my pussy.

The demon nipped at my collarbone before trailing kisses up my neck. My skin burned at his sweet violation as I desperately tried to form a coherent thought. I swallowed thickly as his thumb caressed the folds of my pussy. Spreading them ever so slightly to gain deeper access. *Why does he have to feel so fucking good?*

"Fallon...stop." My words came out as a barely audible whisper, but his movements froze all the same.

Fallon shuddered out a breath. "I can feel how much you want me to, Cinnamon." The sound of my name on his lips almost broke me to pieces. "You don't know how long I've been waiting for someone like you. Just tell me what you need me to do. I'll make it so good for you."

"Let go." My body shook with want; I needed to get away from him immediately. He rested his head against my shoulder before letting out a low growl of frustration. After a deep breath, he released me, only to help steady me as my legs struggled to find purchase on the floor of the carriage. Without bothering to stop the horses, I leaped off and ran to the river to dunk my head in. The cold water shocked most of the desire from my system.

Behind me, I could hear Fallon approach. I held a hand up to stop him. "One hundred points."

"What?"

"Just...just go back to the horses and leave me for a bit, and I'll give you one hundred points."

Without looking back to see if he took the offer, I sat back on the bank for a moment, hiding my head in my hands as I came to a harsh realization: *I'm going to fuck a demon before this is over.*

# Chapter 7

Wandermere was absolutely massive. The streets were alive and crowded with vendors selling their wares and busy people shuffling back and forth. It made my hometown seem incredibly small. Upon entering the gate, Fallon and I (mostly Fallon) received several odd looks. However, we were waved in all the same. I half expected a bit of resistance traveling into a town with a demon at my side, but perhaps things in the cities worked a bit differently.

One woman was shouting about the exorbitant prices of a vendor's exotic furs. The shopkeeper looked rather bored with the entire conversation, but I couldn't help but notice the strange pelts that lined his stand. The animal furs seemed almost unreal. Many of them had several tails, while others had patterns I had never seen.

Fallon scanned the sizable crowd and grit his teeth. "I smell several other demons in this area. But I don't see them anywhere."

"No one seems to be in a panic, so I'd wager a guess that the city is not under attack. Maybe it's just a few smaller ones that got in?" I asked.

Fallon wore an agitated expression as he continued to scan the bustling city around us. "We should be careful, just in case. Something doesn't feel right."

*Vague.* "Alright, I say we find a tavern and catch our breath."

I pointed to a wooden stake with several directional signs. The first three pointed to the town hall and several street names, which meant nothing to me. But the last four seemed to point to places more helpful to travelers. Number four pointed straight ahead to the market, while five read "Pillage and Chill," which…I assumed was a brothel? But six and seven were thankfully advertisements for two taverns named "The Worthless Gazelle" and "The Dramatic Hyena." "Who is naming these businesses?"

"What is a hyena?" Fallon asked.

"I have no idea." Both signs pointed right, so I steered the carriage down the broad road. The streets were built wide enough to comfortably fit two carriages side by side. I kept to the right to try to stay out of the way. "Any preference for Worthless or Dramatic?"

My demon shrugged and leaned back in his seat. "Neither

sound all that appealing. Whichever one is closer will do fine."

A plump woman ran to my side of the carriage and slammed her hand down on the seat, causing me to jump. She wore a simple, off-the-shoulder blouse with a brown corset with yellow accents running up the sides. The bright yellow skirt she wore gave a lovely contrast to her dark complexion. Her rosy cheeks flushed, and she tried to catch her breath.

"Excuse me, lass!" she exclaimed. "If it's a tavern you be wanting, then there is no better place than The Dramatic Hyena! Those Cumberworlders at The Worthless Gazelle will have you sleeping on flea-infected cots. Assuming you survive the slimy plague trap they call food!"

*That's an aggressive sales pitch if I've ever heard one.* "OK, I'm fine with the Dramatic—"

"NOT SO FAST!" came a shout from the other side of the carriage.

"Oh, what now?" Fallon scowled at the young man, who began walking on his side. He, too, wore a white shirt. But his vest and pants were a deep purple. The newcomer glared daggers at the woman as if she were evil incarnate.

"Unless you like slobber in your soup, don't bother with those dullards at the Dramatic Hyena!" This had the plump woman turning a dark shade of red that matched her fiery hair as she bared her teeth at the man. Her adversary in purple took his eyes off her to give me a winning smile. "Your pet demon will have to stay in the barns, of course, but we have some of our finest rooms open!"

*Oh no.*

"Pet?" Fallon's voice was calm, but the question sent a chill to my bones. *Do these crazy people actually keep demons as pets?* I did not know how that was even possible. My brothers visited the city all the time to sell our spices, and not once did they ever mention seeing a werewolf walking around on a freaking leash. Any time a monster came too close to Boohail, the village guards drove it off or killed it. Minus Fallon. But my villain-adjacent would have just sent them into an early grave.

The Hyena advocate threw back her head and laughed. "Ha! Some customer service you lot have!" She patted my leg as if we were old friends and grinned. "Come stay with us, love. I'll even throw in a shiny new collar for your demon. He hasn't got one on—wouldn't want the town guard to see that. It's a hefty fine if you cross a guard looking to line his pockets. Not that I think the government should have any more say on how we keep our things in line."

"Oh, did you hear that, Rabbit? A shiny new collar!" His voice took on a chipper note, and I got a distinct feeling if these two idiots didn't shut up, it would be the last argument they ever had.

The woman cocked her head at him. "Did that demon just talk?"

*Shit. Can the captured demons not talk? Come to think of it, I've never heard of an intelligent beast before.* I was a kid the last time Volsog gate opened. A few weaker demons had slipped into my village, but they were dealt with quickly enough. I for sure don't recall any of them talking.

I raised my hand to cut in, but the Gazelle advocate continued. "Oh, of course you'd let filthy demons run loose in your tavern! Just like you do with that disgusting hyena!" He turned back to me and gave a thumbs up. "Don't listen to her. Your demon will be plenty comfy in our stables. You can even pet our dear mascot gazelle!"

"Nobody wants to pet your stupid Gwendolyn, Tyrice!" his adversary hollered back. I guess her feud was more critical than the possibility of Fallon talking.

Tyrice's eyes grew wide in shock. "You keep her name out of your thin mouth!"

"OK!" I shouted, needing to put an end to this. "Ma'am, please take us to the Dramatic Hyena." I turned to Tyrice and shook a finger at him. "You shouldn't make anyone stay in a stable. It's not only poor business; it's just discriminatory." He gave me an incredulous look, but huffed off.

The woman grinned and slammed her fist on the seat again. "A fine choice, lass!" she exclaimed.

Taking Fallon's clenched fist in my hand, I leaned in to whisper so the woman couldn't hear. "I don't know what their problem is, but we won't be here long. Just try to stay calm for now."

He closed his eyes for a moment to cool his features. His shoulders relaxed, but when he opened his eyes again, you could see the thinly veiled rage underneath. It would have to do for the time being.

"Um, ma'am?" I called to the tavern woman leading the way.

"The name's Usha, dear," she chirped back.

"Usha, would you mind telling me why my companion needs a collar?" The woman seemed like the honest sort. Any information I could get out of her would be a massive help. Cumin never bothered to talk about how things were run when he'd go to Wandermere to deliver our goods. He only liked telling us whatever mischief he'd got into.

Usha turned back with a confused look. "Not from around here, are ya?"

"No, I'm from Boohail."

She made a turn down a less busy road. The endless shops gave way to tiny houses and the occasional pub.

"Boohail, huh? That explains it," Usha said, nodding. "The pet demons round these parts have to wear a collar stating who owns 'em. Just in case the holding magic pops off, and one starts biting. Gotta know who to blame, ya know?"

"Ah, the holding magic. Of course, well, I'd be grateful for a collar and room then." I could feel Fallon bristle beside me, so I held his hand tighter and hoped he could keep it together.

If these people had a way to control demons, this city would be more dangerous than I thought. Fallon blowing his top and setting the place on fire was the last thing anyone needed. The sooner we got what we came for and got out, the better.

"Do you happen to know where the temple is? I'd like to pay my respects tomorrow."

"You country folk are a devoted bunch, aren't ya?" she said, smiling. "The temple is on the east side of the city near the town hall. If you take the main road back to the city center, the signs will guide you from there."

Usha stopped in front of a three-story building with brick walls on the first level. The other two stories looked like a cozy yellow cottage with red painted shutters and a sloped red roof. Above the door hung a sign with what I assumed was a hyena drinking a large pint of ale. Off to the side was a stable accented with the same colors.

"Here she is!" Usha stated proudly. "The finest tavern this side of Wandermere!"

Behind us, I heard a man scoff. "Yes, if you like chattering ninnies and runny marinara sauce." I turned around to see Tyrice leaning against a purple-painted tavern across the street.

Fallon and I shared a look. "Are you kidding? The two taverns are right across the street from each other?" No wonder they fought constantly. Tyrice leered at us as though we were now enemies across a battlefield. To him, I suppose we were. The Worthless Gazelle proudly hung its own mascot above the door. In the window, I could see a wooden sign that read, "THE HYENA'S POT-ROAST IS SO UNDERCOOKED IT'S STILL MOOING!"

*Damn. That grudge runs deep.*

"Don't listen to that old fool," Usha said, waving him off. "Stable your horses, then come see me at the counter. I'll have your room ready shortly." With that, she rushed inside.

Through the window, I could see her pick up a wooden sign of her own and scribble something down before putting it in the window: "KOLE FERRY'S NOSE IS SO DEEP IN THE HAPPY DUST HE CAN'T SNIFF A WARTHOG'S ASS FROM A ROSE BUSH!"

Upon reading the sign, Tyrice grew beet red and stomped his foot. "You leave my father out of this; you don't know what he's been through!"

Without missing a beat, Usha opened the window and shouted, "Coke! He's been through a lot of coke!"

When I was a little girl, my favorite adventure story was Troy and the Ogre King. Troy was a valiant knight tasked with defeating the evil ogre, King Throllkog. The dastardly ogre had stolen several fair maidens and kept them high in his keep at the top of a mountain. The easiest way for Troy to infiltrate his keep was to disguise himself as a fair maiden in a long, flowing dress and get kidnapped. Naturally, because it was just a story, his plan worked. All the girls were saved, and he was hailed as a true hero. I wonder, however, how hard it was for his companions to get him to put the damn dress on. I felt like I was stuck on that part of the story.

Fallon backed farther away from me, like a jungle cat trapped in a cage. The simple leather collar I held in my hand could have been a deadly poison for how dramatic he was acting. Fitting, since we were staying at the Dramatic Hyena. "Please?"

He took another step back. "Rabbit, I will burn the city to the ground before I put that collar on."

*So we're back to Rabbit then.*

"Look, we only have to be here long enough to destroy the next chalice. We can't do that if you get arrested as soon as you step outside."

We'd been at this all morning. Usha, true to her word, had given me a collar along with the room the night before. She also had my name engraved on the outside, in case Fallon wandered off somewhere. I completely understood his hesitations. It was undignified and ridiculous, but no one said the trip would be easy.

"Or I could just level this whole city and everyone in it on our way to the temple. That way, we wouldn't have to play their ridiculous games. Or are you honestly going to tell me you have sympathy for slavers?" He spat the last word out like a curse.

Despite my best efforts, a small crack appeared in my diplomacy armor. "Listen, dammit, I'm doing the best I can here.

Seeing as how I don't even want to be here...no, I obviously don't care if a bunch of slavers die, but can you confidently say that you can take on a city of slavers with an unknown amount of demons under their control? Are you that confident?"

I stomped to the small window in our room and pulled back the curtains. "If you are, by all means fire away."

He hesitated as he processed my statement, then clenched his teeth in frustration. "When this is over, I have no intention of showing mercy on these humans."

"Once the spell is broken, I imagine you'll have to get in line after every other demon in the city."

After speaking with Usha, I had learned that the ports of Wandermere exported a lot more than just the spices my family sold in town. The mages in this city had found a way to tack on another caveat to the false goddess' curse, making demons subservient to their masters. The capture process was deadly and arduous, so very few knew how to do it, and an even smaller few knew how to put it back on once a demon broke free of it. That was why the collars were so important. If some fool couldn't keep their pet under control, it could rampage and destroy an entire city block.

Fallon ran a hand through his long black hair, sighing heavily and snatching up the collar. "Let's get on with it then."

He strode past me, opening the door, only to find Usha listening behind it. The innkeeper reared back in surprise, almost spilling the two bowls of soup she held on a tray.

She straightened herself and looked up at Fallon, wide-eyed. "Oh, hello there! I just...just thought you two might be hungry, so I brought up a bit of soup!" Usha thrust the tray forward to Fallon's chest and gave a nervous laugh.

When he made no move to take it, she fidgeted more. "How much of that did you hear?" Fallon asked.

Usha swallowed thickly. "Um...all of it. All the bits about destroying a chalice, burning the city to the ground, and ah...a false goddess, was it? Not fans of Myva are ya? I admit she's not much of a hands-on goddess but—"

I jumped to grab the demon's arm when I noticed him grip the hilt of his sword. Usha screamed and backed up, hitting her back against the wall in the hallway. "Rabbit, let go," he warned darkly.

I kept both arms wrapped firmly around his sword arm and shook my head. "Let's all just calm down and breathe for a moment! No need for anyone to be swinging any swords. Usha, I swear I can explain everything!"

After shoving Fallon aside, I filled in Usha on the hell-scape that my life had been for the past week. The woman sat on the only bed occupying the room and stared off into space. She opened her mouth as if to say something, then thought better of it.

"You OK, hun?" I asked, petting a hand on her shoulder.

Fallon ignored us both, choosing instead to help himself to the soup left abandoned on the table.

She took a deep breath and blinked. "Well, of course!" she said, smiling. "I mean, the goddess is fake, your demon can talk like a normal man, and my whole life is a lie, but sure! I'm dandy!" Nervous laughter caused her body to shiver.

"Do you maybe need a minute?"

She stood and brushed herself off. "No, no. What's done is done." She shook out her hands and approached Fallon at his seat on the table. He looked up at her with a bored expression but kept eating. "You...can talk," she began slowly. "And... and not just basic words either. Like rational spoken words?"

"I tend to save my mindless screaming for Tuesdays," he replied coolly.

Usha brought a hand to her cheek in a nervous motion before smoothing her skirts again. "OK, so it would stand to reason that you and other demons like yourself have complex thoughts. Hopes and dreams, just like we do. Not...not just mindless beasts?"

Fallon rolled his eyes and rested his head on his hand. "It would seem so."

"Oh dear." The innkeeper began to pace back and forth.

Maybe I should have just lied and said Fallon was a particular case, so we could have just left her out of it. Though there was no guarantee that he wouldn't kill her just to keep her quiet. Usha was eccentric but had been nothing but kind to us since we got there.

After a moment, she stomped her foot and marched up to

Fallon again. Then, with a deep breath to steel her nerves, she bowed her head. "I'm sorry!"

"What?" we asked in unison.

Usha kept her head bowed as she replied. "I'm sorry. While I didn't take any slaves of my own, I thought nothing was wrong with the practice. I thought demons were just mindless animals, and that was wrong. If destroying Myva's chalice will break the curse, then I'd like to help you while you are here."

*Oh. That took a turn.*

Fallon rose from his chair and clapped a hand on Usha's shoulder. She flinched and looked up at him. "Thank you," he said simply.

"Hey, Usha, not that I'm complaining, but why are you agreeing to help us?" I asked. Concern crept into the back of my mind. She really had no reason to jump on board so quickly. She didn't even know us.

The innkeeper's smile faded. Her gaze dropped to the floor, and her hands clenched the front of her skirt. "I've unknowingly walked past fully sentient people being treated as less than animals and did nothing. If it were me at the end of a chain, I couldn't imagine the kind of monster that would walk past me and do nothing if they knew the truth."

Her answer left me speechless for a moment. But she was right. Her logic was simple and just made changing one's entire worldview seem like a mundane occurrence. *Maybe it should be. As much as I'd rather stay out of conflict and live out my* life in peace, I don't think I could walk away from someone suffering in front of me.

"So," Usha began, turning to me. "What's the plan?"

*Right. People typically have those in this sort of situation. OK, let's think.* "How heavily guarded is the temple? Can the average person just walk in?"

The innkeeper tilted her head to the side in thought. "You can; however, the temple is attached to the mage's hall. They come and go through the temple all the time. I doubt they'd be too keen on you breaking the chalice. Any demon larger than a small imp isn't permitted to even be near it. It's not uncommon for tourists to walk in, though."

"If any mages get in the way, I'll just kill them." Fallon grinned at the thought. Usha stepped a little further away from him. I couldn't really blame her.

I rolled my eyes at the demon and shook my head. "No. First off, you can't even enter the temple until the protective magic is disturbed. Second, we don't fully know how those mages put demons under their control, even if you could. Third, the cinnamon you carry may not be enough to protect you."

Fallon clenched his fists and gave a frustrated sigh. "Well, I'm not sending you in there alone. If she sends her undead to protect her phylactery like the last time, I'll need to be there to protect you."

*Aw, the big guy cares.*

Usha resumed her pacing once more, as she held her chin.

After a moment, her head popped up, and she spun around to grin at us. "Maybe Cin doesn't have to!"

"What are you thinking?" I asked.

She rubbed her hands together in delight. "The carriage you two came in, it looks just like your average merchant cart!"

"Well, it is," I said, not sure where this was going.

"Exactly! I could drive your cart down to the mage hall to sell some of your wares. I'm familiar with them, so they won't suspect me. Fallon could hide in the back while you run in and snag the chalice!"

I jumped off the bed in excitement. "Myva may not know what's going on until I actually try to smash it! If we can break it before the sorcerers even know Fallon is in the cart, we may just have a chance!"

"But are they just going to let you walk out with it?" Fallon asked.

My shoulders slumped. "Shit."

"They won't know it's gone," Usha said, grinning. "You can find a replica of the goddess' chalice in the market square. Tourists eat that kind of thing up. Switch it up with the real one while I make a bit of noise outside. I'll have Kiki kick up a fuss or something."

"Who's Kiki?" I hadn't seen any other workers since we got there. The inn was relatively small. I assumed she meant her sister.

Usha poked her head in the hallway and made a "whoop whoop" sound. A stomping noise followed before a strange beast entered the doorway, tail wagging. It looked like a dog put together with spare parts. The creature's back was sloped down with a hunch at the shoulder blades. Its face was short, with a massive set of teeth that rivaled that of a jaguar. The beast's head came up to Usha's chest as it leaned in so she could scratch its face. She rubbed her hands through its shaggy fur, which had long stripes starting at the middle of its back and tapering off to spots where it reached the creature's belly. Horrifying. Kinda cute, when I squinted, but mostly horrifying.

"This is our mascot, Kiki!" the innkeeper said proudly. "She's a short-faced hyena, and she never fails to get a laugh out of a crowd."

Kiki eyed Fallon and me for a moment before letting her tongue loll out of her mouth in a silly grin. Seeing such a stupid face on a monster-sized creature was so ludicrous, I couldn't help but laugh. To my utter shock, Kiki laughed back.

Fallon snorted behind me as the laughter spread to him. "I've never seen such a ridiculous creature."

The beast threw back her head and laughed harder, as if she agreed.

Usha beamed at us. "See! The crowd never stands a chance."

## Chapter 8

One of the market stalls was cooking up something fierce, and I needed to find it. The smell of meats and cheese nearly had me floating in a trance towards its call. Usha and Fallon agreed to set up their position at the temple an hour before I did to avoid suspicion. That meant I had a bit of time to kill and an empty enough stomach to know what to do with that time.

Luckily, Usha wasn't kidding when she said finding a fake chalice would be the most straightforward bit. As soon as you walked into the marketplace, eager vendors sniffed out tourists like wolves on fresh meat. I was no exception.

After I looked around at a few shops at the entrance, an eager old woman with a grip like a bear trap all but hauled me into her store. She held every manner of knick-knacks, including the needed chalice. In multiple colors, I might add. The people of Wandermere did not mess around when it came to selling their wares.

Once my decoy was placed neatly in my satchel, I excused myself from the woman before she could convince me that I did, in fact, need a new dress, pretty shoes, and a fancy hat.

My stomach roared its war cry when I stopped in front of the food stall that had been sending out that delicious aroma. Above it, the word "Nachos" was written in bold letters. My brother had mentioned eating that when he came here, but I'd never tried the dish myself.

"What will it be, lady?" said a large redheaded man over the counter.

*Crap, I haven't read the menu yet.* "I'll have a nacho, please."

He raised an eyebrow at me. *Do they not come in singular?* The man sighed and asked, "Do you want the small or the bucket?"

"It comes in a bucket?" I was astonished. "Yes, one bucket, please!"

The man grunted and took my coins. He disappeared briefly before returning with what dreams are made of. Triangle-shaped corn chips were mixed together in a pile of ground meat and cheese. A rag was tied to the handle of the bucket, no doubt to save a customer from the horrid mess the masterpiece could make.

I thanked the man with reverence and continued walking

down the marketplace. One bite into the bucket of desires was almost enough to make the entire journey worthwhile. I shoveled my food in with ladylike grace, and meandered through the area. Wandermere had signs guiding you in every direction, so I had no worry of getting lost.

A pained groan shook me out of my food haze.

"Transform, you rotten fleabag!"

Outside of a tanner shop, a portly dark-haired man drew back a whip and brought it down on a tied-up man in front of him. I gasped in horror as the man cried out. The offender raised the whip once more.

"Stop that! What the hell are you doing to that poor man?"

I raced over to them but stayed just out of reach of the man's whip. If he didn't stop, I decided I would toss the bucket at him before tackling him to the ground if needed.

The heavy man scowled in my direction. "Man? Child, it's just a demon. I'm trying to get this werewolf to transform so I can get its coat." He gestured to the tanner shop, whose shelves hung beautiful furs.

Like the shops at the entrance to the city, I couldn't recognize the pelts from any animal I'd seen before. One, in particular, was a lush gray coat with ivory-colored spikes running down the back. Another was so black, it looked like a void to another dimension.

*Oh gods.*

The furs I admired at the entrance to Wandermere were

demon pelts. My gut churned at the thought of walking right past them and not even noticing.

The man on the floor groaned in pain as fresh blood poured from the wounds on his face. Beautiful blond hair hung over his eyes. There was so much blood and filth on him, I almost mistook him for a brunette. He breathed heavily as his head whipped around, as if searching for the assailant right in front of him. Long canines flashed in the sunlight as he growled nonsense words into the air. His body was heavily muscled, just like Fallon, though the stranger seemed a bit smaller. Still, if it were not for the restraints binding him down, I had no doubt he would tower over his attacker.

The whip cracked against his face and he fell to the ground with a sickening thud. "His pelt is no good to me if he won't transform!" the tanner roared before kicking the werewolf.

It was sickening. Even if the man on the ground was a demon, I didn't understand how another man beat someone like that. Destroying the cursed cup would be no good to this werewolf if he were already dead.

"How much is his pelt worth?" I asked, trying to keep my burning rage in check.

The tanner paused his movement before sneering at me. "What do you care for, lass? Don't tell me you think this thing is a man just cause he looks like one. Don't be daft, child."

Straightening my back, I glared back at him. "I know what

a damn demon is. It's his strength that I want." I walked over to inspect the man on the ground. "It would be a waste to kill a beast like this. He'd do well working on my farm." My words felt like acid in my mouth, but if they stopped the madness before me, I decided I could suck up. "How much for him?" I asked, turning back to the fat man.

He rubbed his stubby hand over his beard. "A farmhand, huh? I guess werewolves have a lot of strength to 'em." He sighed and turned his nose up at the broken man on the floor. "This pain in the arse is already giving me more trouble than he's worth, anyway. So tell you what, lady, fifteen silvers, and he's yours."

I scoffed. "Fifteen? The larger pelts in your window are no higher than eight! This wolf's already damaged. Try seven." Of course, haggling was a necessary evil for any merchant—but that tanner was out of his mind if he thought I'd fall for that.

The tanner crossed his arms and nodded to the man on the ground. "The pelts in the window aren't blond. I figure a rare color like that would fetch twice the price!"

"You are crazier than a jaguar on caapi roots if you think you'd get that price for a pelt you've already put marks on." I waved a hand over the lash marks covering the werewolf.

The tanner spat and cursed. "Fine. Eleven silvers, and I'll throw in the lamia I got this morning. He's even bigger than this one. I'd wager he'd do just fine on whatever labor you throw at him."

*What the hell is a lamia? Doesn't matter. Saving two demons is better than one.* "You've got a deal," I said, reaching for my coin purse. It jingled heavily as I dumped out eleven shiny coins into the man's hand.

He grinned before reaching into his pocket and taking out a small blue stone. "Here's the master stone to the wolf. I'll go fetch the other one from the back." With that, he hurried off into his shop, leaving me alone with the werewolf outside.

I rushed to the fallen man's side before pulling out a bag of cinnamon and waving it under his nose. He jerked away as if offended by the smell. "Just keep quiet and bear with it. I'm trying to help you," I whispered to him. Piercing blue eyes flashed up at me before losing focus again. Quickly, I took a pinch of the spice and rubbed it straight against his nose. He sneezed frantically, so I backed off. "Can you understand me now? If you can, I need you to remain calm and play along."

The blond coughed and moved into a sitting position. "I... I can hear you." His voice was low and strained. I did not know how long the poor guy had been captured, but I'd never seen a man in worse shape.

"Good, I'm going to untie you, so don't kill me." Then, moving to his side, I took out a pocket knife and cut the ropes binding his hands and feet. He sighed in relief and began rubbing his chafed wrists. "I'll take your collar off when we're out of the city."

The wolf eyed me like I'd snap on him any second. "Why are you doing this?"

*That has to be the saddest question I've ever heard in my life.*

"Because it's the right thing to do."

The creak of footsteps on wooden floors alerted me to the tanner. "Act like you're still a captive. He's coming back," I hissed. The wolf lowered his head to shield his eyes as I stood back up.

"Well, here he is, told you he was a big one." The tanner seemed a bit out of breath as he exited his shop, tugging on a rope lead. I could see a tall man with long white hair dip low at the door to the shop to avoid hitting his head against the frame. His features were breathtakingly sharp and masculine. His olive skin looked delicate as it stretched over his muscled torso. My eyes shamefully traveled further down to a...fucking nightmare. The man's torso ended in the long white body of a giant snake. He slithered closer to me, led by the tanner. Every fiber of my being told me to turn tail and run.

*What the hell. Why a snake?*

The tanner deposited another stone into my hand and gave me the rope.

*Oh, my filé powder. There's a giant snake man at the end of this rope. Oh my swamp spiders, why me?*

Refusing to show fear, I tore my eyes off the snake beast to nod at the tanner.

"I'll be off then," I said succinctly. "Let's go, wolf."

Behind me, I could hear the blond man grunt and stumble to his feet. My own legs were heavy as stone as I tried to get them to turn and walk away. I know you shouldn't judge a book by its cover, but I was terrified of snakes! They're so long, you never see them coming, and they do that weird flick thing with their tongue!

*Damn it all. Focus up, Cin.*

I kept my gaze on the street ahead, doing my best to ignore the sound of the snake man slithering at the end of the rope. We walked past a few more shops before I found a quiet enough alley to speak to my two new companions. I ushered the two men further down before guiding the wolf to sit on one of several wooden boxes stacked against a stone wall. Then, taking out my water canteen, I handed it to him along with the rest of my bucket of nachos. "Try to eat a little. It should help build your strength back up."

The blond man's eyes looked unfocused and tired, but he bit into the first chip all the same. Then, after swallowing down some water, his appetite seemed to pick up. Soon he tore into the rest of the food with a vengeance.

"OK, maybe not so fast? You might throw up."

He looked up at me for a moment before grunting and slowing down.

My heart beat faster as I tried to steel myself to deal with my second companion. Finally, swallowing hard, I turned around and looked up at the snake man towering over me.

His eyes were a light gray and completely blank. His head faced in my direction as if waiting for something—but it was clear to me that there wasn't a thought in his head. Was this the full extent of the holding magic? I waved a hand in front of his face but received no reaction.

"He won't move unless you give him an order." The wolf paused to take another sip of water. "Lamias are notoriously vicious. I wouldn't be surprised if those damn mages tried to wipe his mind completely to gain compliance."

Cold chills ran down my spine. "Notoriously vicious," I said weakly. "Oh, how great."

My hands shook as I reached for the cinnamon pouch at my hip. I held it in my hands for a moment as I tried to work up the nerve to bring it to the snake man's face.

"You're still going to free him? He's a lamia."

I turned to see the blond eyeing me with an unreadable expression. He sat stone still on his box as if trying to see through me. I guess that was to be expected. It would be weird to trust a stranger you just met—especially since I was human, just like the people who had captured him.

I growled in frustration and shook myself off. Fallon said that demons always pay off their debts. If I freed this lamia, then I should at least be allowed to live, right? Goddess, I hoped so.

My shaking hands brought the cinnamon up to the lamia's nose. If I could focus on the sculpted features of his face, maybe the rest of him wouldn't be so terrifying. His cheekbones were high and proud around an aquiline nose, with slanted eyes that reminded me of the gray skies of a coming storm. His skin was unbelievably smooth. Maybe if I got on his good side, he'd tell me what the secret was to such perfection. Honestly, if I had that kind of complexion, I'd be an arrogant menace to society.

The man wrinkled his nose slightly but didn't move. Impatient woman that I am, I opened the bag further and bopped his nose with it, leaving cinnamon all over his nose and mouth. This caused the desired coughing fit, so I took a few steps back and let the man sort the curse out of his system.

In a flash, the lamia whipped around as a horrible hiss ripped from his throat. His eyes grew slanted like a predator ready to strike. I stumbled back in fear, but my scream was cut off by the snake end of his body coiling itself around me. It squeezed so tight I could barely breathe. I gasped for air as the lamia drew me closer. His rage-filled eyes glared at me with so much disdain I thought I'd burst into flames.

"Um, hello. Nice of you to join us," I croaked out as tears sprung up in my eyes. "Please don't eat me."

"Let her go, snake." The werewolf jumped up with a lopsided grin on his face. "She just freed us both."

My captor's eyes widened at the werewolf before he looked back at me with a stern expression. "Why?" His voice was deep and full of threat, which only caused me to tear up more. *Gods, snakes are scary.*

His scaly body tightened further until I could hear my back pop. "My...my name is Cinnamon. I'm a spice farmer traveling with another demon to destroy Myva's phylactery. He wants to kill her for good, and I'm honestly fine with that cause she seems like a real prick. I freed you because slavery is wrong. I'm also terrified of snakes and being squeezed to death, so please let go!"

After a moment, the vice grip on my body loosened as I was lowered to the floor. Air flooded back into my lungs as I gasped for breath. I sank to the floor in relief. My whole body still shook with fear, so I took deep breaths and tried to calm down.

The snake lowered himself down until he was about eye level with me. I leaned back, and my breath caught, unsure of what he might do. He lifted his hands and fidgeted for a moment, his brows furrowed. I stood frozen. He closed his eyes and lunged forward.

I yelped as his arms came around me, bringing me against his chest. *A hug?* I looked up to the werewolf for answers, but he shook his head and shrugged. *Um...OK.* I slowly hugged him back, not sure if that's what he wanted.

When we pulled back, his face was much softer. His eyes lost their predatory slit. "I didn't expect to be saved by a human. I apologize for attacking you."

"It's fine." The change in attitude had me a little flustered, but I welcomed it. For a minute, I'd thought I was snake food.

The werewolf brushed past him and pulled me to my

feet. He grinned and bowed slightly. "Good to meet you, Miss Cinnamon. My name is Felix. Not sure what convinced a nice girl like you to join forces with a demon, but you can count me in."

That caused me to perk up. The more people we had to drive off the mages, the better. "Really? I'm on my way to the temple to steal the goddess' chalice now. If you want to help, I'm sure we'll need a hand to fight off the mages."

Felix grinned even wider, showing off sharp canines. "Cin, if you think I'm going to miss out on the chance to rip those mages to shreds and crush their beating hearts in my hand, you are very wrong."

I nodded. "Cool, cool. Graphic, but I'll take it." I turned to the lamia. "Are you going to be alright on your own, or would you like to come along? You don't have to fight if you don't want to."

The snow-haired man's eyes darkened with a chilling glint. "We lamia have haunted the dreams of men since the time of the ancients. The grandchildren of those who hurt me will weep at the sound of my name after I throw them in the pyre of my hatred and dance in the rain of their ashes."

"Oh." *That's…a lot to take in.* "Well. You guys are fun." I clasped my hands together before they started to shake again. "Does the ancient terror have a name, or should I just call you Dances In Ashes?"

Felix snorted as he ate another nacho.

"Ambrose," the lamia said, smiling. If it wasn't for the bone-chilling declaration he just made, I'd almost find it a friendly grin.

*This is so much more than I signed up for.*

"Nice to meet you, Ambrose and Felix. Let's get this horror show on the road."

On our way to the temple, Ambrose and Felix agreed to keep their collars on and wait just outside the mage zone until I was ready to signal them once I had the chalice. I was surprised at their agreeable nature after traveling with Fallon the past few days. Maybe I had just been unlucky with my first introduction to demon men.

When we drew closer to our destination, there was a significant increase of men and women in creepy black robes. Judging by the loosely concealed reptilian rage coming off the lamia, I guessed the creepy cult guys were mages. They paid us little mind, most likely thanks to the collars. One held up a rather ominous sign that read: "Goddess loves you. Dave loves you. Dave is love." I leaned closer to Felix to ask who Dave was, but he was just as clueless.

Up ahead, a thick red rope formed a fence barring entry to the mage zone of the city. Two guards dressed in steel plate armor guarded the only entrance. "I think this is where I leave you two." Ambrose squeezed my shoulder gently before he and Felix departed.

*OK. I can do this. Just walk past the guards like a normal person.*

Through the tiny visors in their face armor, I wasn't even sure if the guards could see me. But as I passed by them, neither one so much as twitched. "Well, that was easy," I muttered to myself. *Too easy.* I looked around the mage's square, trying to spot any grand mage ready to jump out and kill me for trespassing. The streets were just full of regular-looking cloaked mages with the occasional tourist.

To the left of the square was a path leading down to the ports. In the distance, I saw several large ships in the bay. At the center of the court was a beautiful fountain with a statue of Myva in the center. She held one of her sacred chalices and poured water in a rush below. Behind it was a wide marble staircase leading to the temple itself. Like the temple of Boohail, it was a modest marble structure the size of a small house. Four columns stood proudly at the entrance, whose doors were wide open to receive visitors.

On the left and right of the temple were two massive Gothic buildings that stood at least five houses high. Two towers reached the skies on both sides of the buildings, while the base held an entrance with arched black doors. Above them sat a beautiful stained-glass window. The windows of both buildings seemed to depict the story of Myva arriving in a demon-ravaged land on the left, while the right showed humans bowing to her after she sealed the demons behind Volsog gate. *Conceited much?*

Much to my relief, I spotted Usha in front of the building on the right. She was shouting something about a spice deal while her hyena danced in front of a crowd of mages. Compared to them, I was utterly invisible to those around me. "Was this actually going to work without a hitch?" I whispered to myself. It was hard not to get my hopes up, but the hope of catching a break was too strong.

I walked right into the temple past several mages chatting idly about some flying spell. To play the part of a wandering tourist, I took the time to look around the area before approaching the chalice in the center. The plain wooden cup was identical to the one I had destroyed before. Only this time, I packed a hammer to make it easier to break.

The three chatting mages were still at the front of the building. That must have been the catch. I couldn't just swap out the chalice with them standing there. I debated the option of just trying to smash the real chalice before they could get to me. But the first cup didn't exactly shatter with just a tap —the wooden monstrosity would take a few hits until it gave. If Myva summoned more of her undead beasts to help stop me, then I would need Fallon to back me up again.

"Holy smokes, that hyena is dancing!" one of the cloaked men shouted.

"What? I want to see!"

With that, my last obstacle was out of the way. *Bless you, Usha.*

Without giving myself time to doubt, I fished the fake chalice out of my bag and swapped it for the real one. Immediately I could feel a pulse of power come from it. Once the cup was off the altar, black sludge bubbled inside of it. So as not to arouse suspicion, I calmly turned around and walked out, humming a tune. I held the bubbling cup behind me as the sludge began to fall to the floor and groan.

I bolted out of the temple as sludge poured from the chalice in my hand. Thinking quickly, I whipped out the cup back behind me so the sludge would fall inside the temple. When I burst into the light outside, a single mage widened his eyes in surprise. "There's a sludge demon attacking Myva's chalice!" I screamed.

The men in black gasped and ran past me into the temple. When I reached the bottom step, the sludge began to form into two bone orcs who looked downright pissed. Veering left, I sprinted toward Usha and Fallon on the other side of the fountain.

I could hear the scream of a man behind me. Soon after, his shrieking body flew just past my head and landed harshly in the fountain.

"You insolent mortal! I will BATHE IN YOUR BLOOD!" Myva screamed from her sludge pile.

The cart where Fallon hid was a mere ten feet away. I called for him, Felix and Ambrose as I ran for all I was worth. One undead orc reached to swipe at me, just grazing my skirt hem.

People screamed in shock as I heard my demon emerge from the cart. I placed the chalice on the edge of the fountain and struck it as hard as I could. The voice of Myva screamed in agony as the cup formed a large crack down the side. Blood and black sludge exploded from the chalice, quickly developing into the putrid bone orc she had used before.

"Get away from me, you wretched girl!" she screamed.

The orc tried to grab me. I jumped away just in time to feel it graze the front of my blouse. It screamed in rage as it shielded the cup from me.

*Shit, shit, I should have grabbed it.*

A second orc formed from the sludge. I looked to Fallon for help, but my demon was tearing through a crowd of mages that had surrounded the cart. The cloaked cult freaks swarmed around him like ants as they shot blue and black magic bolts at him. Fallon roared in fury and swung his sword wide. Flames engulfed the air left behind from his swing, catching four mages in the crossfire. They screamed as the fire overwhelmed them, but more mages just kept pouring in from the two Gothic buildings. I had to cut off the source of their magic, or we'd be goners.

One orc reached for me again, but I dodged and swung at its hand with my hammer. The patched-together hand shattered into a pile of finger bones at the monster's feet. Before it could recover, I dove between its legs and took a mock swipe at the second one. Once it raised its arms to shield its chest, I veered around it and snatched the half-broken chalice from the fountain. More blood spewed from its center, coating my corset in enough muck to give me nightmares for years.

In front of me, my two horses broke free of their reins and panicked in the chaos. True to his namesake, Crash barreled into a trio of mages who were firing spells at Fallon. Glass bottles fell out of the mages' robes and shattered against the pavement. They released green smoke, concealing the mages and my horses from sight. I heard one of the mages scream out, "Goddess dammit, not the flying potions!"

Smash flung herself out of the smoke carried by two giant black wings. She shrieked in fear, knocking into the orc blocking my path. The bone monster went down hard, half of its body breaking against the cobblestone pavement. I took the chance to duck behind the cart, just narrowly avoiding Crash as he too flew out of the mist. He dipped frantically to the side, unsure of how to use his new wings. Unfortunately, the female mage below him was not as lucky as me and took a hoof to the back of the head.

"Focus on the dragon!" one man shouted. "We've almost got him under heel!" More men shouted encouragement as a crowd gathered together.

I scanned the skies for any fire-breathing monsters, but saw no dragon. *What the hell are they talking about?*

Further, I could see a massive white snake strike out into

the fray and swallow a mage whole. Its long body wrapped around two more men in cloaks before squeezing so tightly they burst. Blood shot all over his snow-colored scales. I shivered at the memory of being wrapped in that coil only an hour or so before.

Usha screeched and ran away as two mages tried to tackle her. One managed to grab her around the waist before a yellow werewolf bit him around the neck, forcing him off of Usha and onto the ground.

I held the chalice to the ground and smashed it again with the hammer. Again, more pieces splintered off as the false goddess screamed in agony.

A massive bone hand wrapped around my ankle and hoisted me in the air. I could do nothing but cry out as the remaining orc threw me like a ragdoll into the nearby fountain.

I hit the statue hard on my right side and fell into the water, dropping the cup. Pain blurred my vision as I frantically searched the water for it. My fingers just barely grazed its lip when I felt something grab my other wrist. Snatching the cup, I braced myself as the undead abomination pulled me up by the arm. My feet dangled uselessly as the creature held me to its deformed face. The beast only had small patches of skin on its face. Most of it was bare muscle stretched loosely over bone and sinew. There were no eyes in its sockets, just two dark voids that somehow still managed to look at me. Its mouth held long tusks coming from the bottom jaw. It creaked and snapped as it tried to put itself together to form words. The scent of death rolled off it in waves.

"You think...you can beat me, little girl?" Myva asked through its broken maw. "I am eternal. I am a god!"

"Your breath stinks," I grit out.

I slammed the cup against the orc's tusk with all the force I could muster. Finally, it shattered down the middle before falling uselessly into the water below. The orc disappeared in a black smoke before I dropped back into the fountain with a loud splash.

My whole body ached in pain as I stood on unsteady feet. The water was a disgusting shade of reddish-brown. I couldn't tell if any of the blood in the water was mine. My head felt dizzy as the world spun. I tried to focus on the dark figure coming towards me. My vision attempted to force the two dizzying images to become one as a bright light flashed. More pain shot through me like lightning. There was a high-pitched keening in my ears. When my eyes cleared, I could see my reflection in the filthy water. The sound was me. I was screaming.

"You crazy bitch!" said a man in front of me. He wore the same black cloak as the other mages, but a gold chain hung loosely around his neck. He waved a long crooked wand, and a bright light, followed by more pain, took over me.

I screamed and fell to my knees.

*How long does it take to pass out from pain?*

My whole body was singing with agony, and lord, I could really use the sweet release of darkness.

Then, all at once, the shocking pain stopped. I could hear the man gasp through the ringing in my ears.

"No! No, please!"

Fallon was suddenly right in front of him. Wordlessly, my demon grabbed the man by his head and tore it clean off his shoulders. The body flailed its arms wildly before falling to its knees, then flat on the ground.

*Well, that's gonna leave a mental scar.*

Fallon turned to me then. Instead of the dark coal eyes I'd grown fond of, the cold yellow gaze of a predator rooted me to the spot. He strode toward me with a menacing aura that had me backing away. My back hit the wall of Myva's statue, sending jolts of fear through my already fried nerves.

The demon let out a breath, which turned into small flames around his face. He kneeled in front of me and took my face in his hand. Then, with gentle care mismatched with the anger in his eyes, he turned my head slowly from side to side.

"You're hurt," he said.

"Well yeah," I breathed. "It looks like you took care of that prick, though." A nervous laugh escaped my throat as I noticed Fallon's nails extend into deadly looking claws. He ran a careful hand over my body. Goosebumps spread down the trail his fingers left.

A small smile graced his lips. "Every scratch," he whispered,

133

his tone gentle and comforting, "every bruise, I will pay back in fire and blood."

I blinked. "Um...that is so sweet but so unnecessary," I said to unhearing ears. Fallon had already stood and walked away from me. His large form seemed to vibrate as a black mist swirled around him. The fog grew larger and larger until a bone-chilling roar rocked the very earth beneath me. All at once, the black smoke shot up into the sky until a long, serpent-like form grew out of it. The creature weaved through the air like the night sky, coming to destroy the sun itself. Obsidian hair flowed down the creature's long back as it twisted itself around the entire square. Dangerous curved horns adorned its head in a crown of horror. All around me, the remaining mages screamed and began running out of the court towards the rest of the city. Yellow eyes fixed on the scrambling men.

Despite the flames the dragon sent down into the square, my body felt cold. Disbelief clouded my mind. Fallon was a dragon. I'd been traveling with a fucking dragon.

The world around me drowned in a sea of fire. Through the flames, I could hear people screaming as they disintegrated into ash. With a sweep of his tail, Fallon toppled the mage hall. Myva's beautiful stained glass window shattered into a distant memory.

Usha came to my side and shook me. She screamed something and tried to pull me up but my mind couldn't process whatever was coming out of her mouth. She dragged me to the upturned cart, with Ambrose close behind.

Where was Felix? I screamed for him, looking around to see if anyone else was still alive. When I saw the werewolf emerge unharmed, I teared up with relief. He gave me a lop-sided grin and came to sit next to the rest of us behind the cart. He sighed and leaned back against the coach with a slight smile on his face.

"How are you so calm?" I asked, bewildered. My body shook like a leaf as hell literally rained down around us, and this man looked like he just sat down for tea.

Felix brought a hand up to his neck and tore the collar off like it was parchment paper. "Well, he's not after us, is he, Mrs. Dragon?" He moved closer next to my side. "So long as we're next to his lovely mate, we're as safe as can be."

I shook my head. "I'm not his mate."

Ambrose chuckled. "I'd tell that to your dragon. Not us." He had Usha tucked into his side as he shielded her from the falling embers. The woman's massive hyena cowered at her other side.

"How do we stop him?" I asked, frantic.

The werewolf arched an eyebrow at me. "We? No, no, dear. A werewolf and a lamia do not stop a dragon. You can walk over and see if batting your eyes at him might do the trick. Otherwise, I'm keen to let him burn down the whole cursed city. Serves them right for what they've done."

I glanced over the cart to see Fallon had moved further into the city. He threw back his massive head and burned another tower to the ground. "What about the other demons trapped in there?"

Ambrose peered into the distance as he kept a firm hand on Usha's shoulder. "If they're smart, they'll flee."

The innkeeper huffed and pushed away from Ambrose. "You two are ridiculous." She dusted herself off and grabbed my hand, pulling me up. "Let's go, Cin."

"And do what?" I asked warily.

She rolled her eyes. "You are going to grab your demon before he destroys everything on this side of the continent. I am going down to the docks with these two to pick out our new ship." At my confused expression, she continued. "Hun, we just destroyed the city. We are officially wanted criminals at best. Your horses can fly now, sure, but your cart is smashed, and I doubt we could all escape happily into the sunset on it if it wasn't. A ship, however…"

My head fell in my hands as I let out an aggravated sigh. "I bet Troy and the Ogre King never had to deal with this," I muttered.

"What's that, Cin?" Usha asked.

"Nothing. It doesn't matter anymore, so fuck it. Piracy."

*Chapter 9*

I really wanted a cat. And a man who would love to have picnics with me on Sundays. I wanted to add a sun room on to my house, so Brie and I could drink together without the harassment of mosquitoes. I wanted to see my brothers wrestle with my husband after some silly contest Cumin made up. We could all go down to the river and catch crawdads, talking about everything and nothing. Then, on days with good spring weather, we could laze away on a hill, enjoying the fresh smell of my cinnamon fields. The only thing my man and I would have to worry about, was what we wanted to do for dinner the next day.

Though at that moment, I really would just settle for the cat.

Wandermere was almost completely destroyed. Long stretches of the city lit up like candle sticks anytime the black dragon spewed another gout of flame. The remaining people fled toward the gates, in the opposite direction of me. Not all of them would make it. Disgruntled freed slaves hunted after their old masters, paying no mind to the deathbringer above them. I wondered briefly why not one demon had turned their ire on me. Maybe they just saw a crazy woman walking towards the eye of the storm and assumed I'd die anyway.

I looked up to see Fallon's long body circle around an abandoned coliseum.

The dragon's legs were tucked neatly against his body as it weaved through the air, searching for another target. Two long whiskers adorned the sides of his snout. They danced in the wind, mimicking the movement of the rest of the serpent. Odd how he flew with no wings. Despite the lack of appendages, the dragon commanded the surrounding sky in a breathtakingly beautiful display. If it wasn't for the destruction he was causing, I would have liked to sit and watch him for hours.

Loud banging noises came from a door in the hallway once I entered the marble structure. I made my way over and grabbed the wooden plank holding the door shut.

"Stop pounding the door so I can open it," I shouted to the other side.

Once the banging ceased, I removed the plank and pulled the door open. With a roar, enormous monsters began rushing out into the open air. A beast that looked like the love child of a lion and a man skittered to a halt at the sight of me. A few other demons stopped to look back as well.

"A woman?" The lion-man tilted his head, confused. "And a human woman at that." He was joined by a minotaur and another giant humanoid that may have been a bear-shifter of some sort. They were all dressed in gladiator clothing, with iron collars around their necks. Those must have been too hard to snap off.

"Yeah. I'm with the dragon." I shrugged.

The minotaur stepped closer to sniff me before wrinkling his nose with a snort. "You're covered in mage blood."

"It's been a long day," I said dryly. "Anyway, Myva's chalice has been destroyed. So you all are free to go."

"I suppose that explains why we can think straight for the first time in years," the lion-man grunted.

*Years? Damn. They must have been captured the last time Volsog gate opened.*

"By the way, if you ever have to go near another one of Myva's chalices, the antidote to the madness spell is cinnamon."

I tried to walk away from the demons, but the bear-shifter reached out and grabbed my arm. "Wait. Is the dragon your mate?"

*Not this shit again.*

"If not, I'll claim you. I've never met a woman brave enough to take on a mage." The bear-shifter was shoved by the lion creature, who blocked the last man from seeing me.

"I saw her first, you honey-eating bastard." He turned to smile at me. I took a step back at the sight of his huge fangs.

"You're scaring her, you oaf," the bear-shifter snapped from his spot on the ground. This was far beyond my patience level.

"Gentlemen," I began, raising my hands in a placating manner. "The dragon is my mate, actually. So I'd better get back to him."

A frown settled on the lion's face as he studied me. "I don't smell a mark on you."

The ground shook with a boom as Fallon landed in the center of the coliseum. He lowered his massive head until his chin almost dragged on the ground in front of him. Pitch black lips curled over ivory fangs as he took in the sight before him.

Displeased, the dragon roared, knocking me off my feet. I stumbled forward before grabbing on to a column for support. The three beast-men took the hint and ran out of the building without so much as a glance.

"Have we settled down now?" I asked, walking over to him.

The dragon made a low rumbling sound and kept his eyes locked on the door where the beast-men left. Fallon's head in this form was bigger than my whole body. Small blue-tinted scales covered his face before they branched out into the more extensive armor-like plates that went down the length of his body. I reached out to touch his cheek. It was smooth and warm. He settled his head down to the floor and let out a breath. My hand moved up to his mane, combing through the soft tresses. *Damn him.* His hair was always so pretty, and I knew for a fact he didn't do shit to it. The man didn't even have to use my hair cleanser to get it this smooth.

"You never told me you were a dragon," I said after a moment.

"**It never came up in conversation.**" The voice of a dragon was like someone put a cello in a long cave. Impossibly deep, yet pleasant.

*This guy…*

"Why didn't we just fly here, though?"

He let out a hum and closed his eyes. "**This form is hard to maintain and control. It takes a dragon three hundred years to master it. If I transformed in a place where Myva could control me, there's little I could do to stop her.**"

"That's a long time just to get a handle on your own body. How old are you?"

"**One hundred and twenty-four.**"

"Ah, so you've only got one hundred years on me! You old fart," I teased.

He laughed. The rumbling sound reverberated through the stone columns around us. "**Is that any way to talk to your mate?**"

My cheeks flushed. "I clearly just said that to get away from those other men."

His lips curved over his dagger-like teeth in a wicked-looking grin. "**What's that, my love? I couldn't hear you over the sound of your hands in my hair.**"

141

*Shit.* I froze, then pulled my hands away from him. That set loose another round of rumbling laughter from the dragon as black talons gently closed around my torso. Before I could make a sound, I was lifted into the air. Black smoke billowed around us as I rose higher out of the coliseum and landed on the balcony of a nearby townhouse. Fallon, now in human form, threw me over his shoulder and walked further into the suite.

I let out a squawk at the rough treatment and steadied my hands on his back. The gray shirt he wore was covered in ash, and I couldn't help but wonder where his clothes went when he transformed. "Put me down! I can walk."

He ignored my protests and looked around for a moment before walking down the hall into a washroom. To say the area belonged to the wealthy elite of the city was an understatement. Everything was covered in gold trim. The tub was big enough for five people and lined with rubies, while sapphire filigree adorned the mirrors above the sink.

Pity it was on the fourth floor. It must have taken servants forever to carry water up there. Fallon set me down and walked over to the tub. He pulled on a lever, and a wooden plank dropped down. Water spewed from it directly into the tub.

"How did you do that?" I stared at the contraption in amazement. *That would save so much time every time you wanted a bath! Could every washroom in the city do that?*

Fallon rubbed his eyes and searched the cabinet next to

the bath, and pulled out a jar of soap. "Ah, I forgot you haven't been outside of your village. Most large cities have an intricate water system that can do this sort of thing. I've been in cities that use magic to just carry water everywhere, but it looks like this city has a rather advanced aqueduct system. Though the water looks warm, so maybe there is some magic involved."

"It's warm?" I asked excitedly, dunking my hands under the running water to find it at the perfect temperature. *Well, this is just too good to be true.*

"I'll search the rooms to see if I can find some clothes that are not disgusting. Go ahead and wash off," he said before heading out of the room.

"Hey, Fallon?" He paused at the door. "How do you feel about cats?"

He raised an eyebrow. "They've never bothered me. Why?"

"No reason, just wondering." He shrugged and walked out of the room.

Needing no further invitation, I ripped off my soiled clothing and jumped into the tub. The small fountain pouring water from the top felt like absolute bliss. As the water came down, I noticed a drain at the bottom of the tub. *These city folk think of everything. I could live in this washroom.* The amount of mud and muck I scrubbed off myself was offensive at best. *To think those gladiators still tried to get in my skirts. They're troopers. I'll give them that.*

In the mirrors across from the tub, I could see that my pink hair dye was quickly fading away, returning my curls to their natural dark brown.

*Good riddance,* I thought to myself. *Ever since that stupid dye job, my life has been turned upside down.*

Fallon returned as I rinsed out my hair. He carried a pile of clothes and a few fluffy towels. Placing them on the sink, he made his way over to the tub and began stripping off his clothes. I'd say I didn't stare intensely at the deep V of his hipbones, but Mama didn't raise a liar.

"What, no shock and awe this time?" he asked, standing proud in his nudity.

Too bad for him, I had no intention of giving him the satisfaction of seeing me squirm. I rolled my eyes and went back to rinsing my hair. "Your ego is big enough as it is. I worry if it's fed further, you'll eclipse the sun."

He cocked his head to the side and grinned. "You love it." The demon yawned and dragged himself into the tub.

"You look ready to collapse," I said.

Even slumped over, Fallon was still a head taller than me. He peered at the soap through half-hooded eyes, as if the mere motion of picking it up was a struggle. "As I mentioned, my dragon form is very draining. I'll be fine by tomorrow." His gaze left the soap to stare unabashedly at my chest. The corner of his mouth quirked and he took a step toward me. "Though I could find the strength for other activities."

I leaned in closer and traced my fingers on his bicep. "Well, there is one thing I'd like you to do." Returning his grin, I peered up at him and batted my eyelashes.

The stunned look on his face nearly made me lose my composure, but I held on. He recovered quickly and ran a hand down my side. "What might that be?"

Unable to hold in the giggles any longer, I grabbed him by the horns and guided him to sit under the pouring water. "I want you to take a bath." Then, kneeling down next to him, I moved my lips next to his ear and whispered, "You stink."

Fallon barked out a laugh as the water poured over him. His dark locks clung to his face and back, forming small rivers of ink. I gathered soap in my hands and began working it through his hair. The texture was just as soft as it was in his dragon form. He moved slightly away from the water to make it easier for me to manage.

"So, any other secrets I should know about? You don't have a human-hating brother that's going to show up at some point, do you?"

He shook his head. "No family. It's rare for demons to have any children because of the harsh circumstances in the Northern continent. My parents met their end a long time ago."

"I'm sorry, that must have been lonely."

My brothers were my best friends, with all their annoyances. I couldn't imagine growing up with no siblings to play with. Fallon's overbearing behavior made a little more sense after that. It had probably been a while since he had a companion. My heart went out to the big guy.

"This is new," he remarked, leaning his head into my hands.

I ran my hands through his lengthy locks, taking special care to get the grime out of his ends. "You're exhausted and look ready to keel over. The last thing I need is you passing out and bashing your head on the tile."

He turned toward me. His expression was severe. "Careful, Rabbit, that almost sounded like affection." His face scrunched up at the water I flicked at him.

"You wish," I muttered, moving on to wash his back and shoulders.

The demon grinned like the panther who'd caught the pelican. "Oh, I think it is."

"Someone's confident."

He caught my hand before bringing it up to his face. My breath caught as he placed a gentle kiss on my wrist. "Why did you come to stop me then? You could have taken the chance to run. Yet here you are, washing my back."

My eyes widened at that. Damn demon and his logical thought process. I never even stopped to think about just leaving. It just felt so natural to come back to him. I still missed my home and wanted to go, but my feet led me here.

"I...you know where I live, remember? You could have just found me and hurt my family!" I spat the lie out of my mouth like a curse, and I pulled my hand from him. I got up and backed away, but he turned around and caught my wrist again. He gazed at me with such intensity that I looked away.

Fallon's voice was low, free from his usual playful demeanor. "Do you truly think I could do that to you?"

A knot swelled in my chest as I tried to pull away again. The demon was having none of it. His free hand touched my cheek. The caress was soft, but commanding in its intent. "Cinnamon, look at me. Do you think I would do anything to hurt you?"

No. I knew he wouldn't. But giving in to him was a terrifying thought. As much as my body wanted him, Fallon didn't want casual sex. He wanted forever. I knew he wasn't evil, but he was…dangerous. The peaceful life I had planned for myself would go up in smoke in his hands.

"Don't say my name. It feels weird." The knot in my chest grew as my knees felt weak. Then, when I couldn't look away from him any longer, I felt myself trapped in the harsh intensity of Fallon's obsidian eyes. Gold specs danced around his irises. They were luminescent in a way that outshone every star in the night sky.

His thumb caressed my cheek as he softly spoke, "Answer me, Cinnamon."

The tornado of feelings the small gesture caused in me was dizzying. I needed to get away. It was far too much emotion to handle. Traitorous body that it was, I could feel my eyes begin to water.

"You just leveled half a city!"

"They hurt you," he said as if it was the most obvious thing in the world. "You and every demon in this city. Don't pretend it's the same thing."

I knew that, of course. I shut my eyes, trying to force down the well of emotion. Fallon turned my wrist over before trailing kisses against the sensitive skin, making my breath catch.

"Why won't you just tell me what you're so afraid of?"

If I had met Fallon years ago, before my sister was torn from me, there was a good chance I would have jumped at his offer. A life of adventure with a dragon at my side was better than any of the fairy tales I read as a child. But that Cin was dead.

"You might think I'm interesting now. But what happens when the last cup is broken, and I want to go home to my little quiet life? You're a dragon that kills people with zero hesitation. I'm just a spice farmer! I want lazy days by the river and to drink with my brothers and friends. I want to only have dull and happy days, not go on crazy adventures and possibly steal a ship!" The tears I'd been holding back finally spilled. "And then you'll realize I'm boring and a coward and just leave!"

"Cin. You have never, in your life, been capable of being boring."

I gasped in surprise as Fallon scooped me up from the floor. He hooked an arm around my back and legs. He shifted me against his chest so the demon could use one hand to shut off the faucet. He carried me out of the room, bypassing the clothes he had brought.

"Where are we going?" I asked, wiping the tears from my eyes.

"Well, some fool made the mistake of calling my woman boring. They must be punished." His grin was downright wolfish as he kicked open the door to a bedroom. In three quick strides, he reached the enormous bed in the middle of the room and threw me on it.

"Hey!" I squeaked, trying to right myself.

Fallon climbed on the bed and flipped me onto my back.

"I've never had lazy days by a river," he said as he pulled my legs apart and kissed my inner thigh. The sensation sent a delicious thrill up my body. "I can't say I've had the time or the luxury to consider what you would call a boring life either." I let out a gasp as he ran a hand up my body to grab my breast. "But I do like to drink. When I saw you in the kitchen window, I thought to myself, 'What it must be like to have a family that close. I've never had these things. I don't know how I'd acclimate to them.' But I know that when I look at you, it makes me want to try."

I tried to sit myself up and push him away. "Fallon, wait, I—"

A firm hand pushed me back down onto the plush mattress. He moved up my body to trap my wrists in his hand. He leaned over to snatch a throw blanket from the bottom of the bed before quickly looping it around the bedpost. He brought the ends down to bind my wrists.

"Hold on!" I cried in protest, trying to release the bindings.

Fallon let out a dark laugh before cupping my face in his hand. "I know, I know, love. You've convinced yourself you have to say no to this." He leaned down to kiss my forehead before running his tongue against my neck. "I can see that mind of yours running a mile a minute with excuses. I'm a dangerous demon, and it's wrong for you to want me." I bit back a moan when he nipped at my collarbone. "What if we want different things? What if you're making a mistake?" he continued. His thumb flicked over my nipple until the bud hardened. He brought his face up to mine. The masculine scent of him made my mind dizzy. "But I also see how hungry you are for me. So how about an excuse to say yes?"

A devious smile touched the corners of his mouth before grabbing my neck and squeezing just slightly. The sensation gave me a sinking, helpless feeling. To my surprise, heat pooled in my belly, burning away any sense I had left. "What if the evil demon seduced you away from your better judgment?" Warm lips graced my ear, making me shiver. "I can be your villain," he whispered. "Why don't you let me take away the burden of choice for a while?"

I'd…never been so turned on in my life.

Fallon waited, still as a statue above me. He was still giving me a chance to back out.

*Dammit. Damn him and damn me for wanting him so much.*

I nodded yes.

He shook his head. "I want to hear you say it."

*Damn him.* "Yes."

"Good girl." His voice was deep and rich, like chocolate drizzled over cake.

My demon bent down and kissed me gently at first as if to test my reaction. But when I licked his bottom lip, he cupped my face in his hand as his tongue coaxed my own out from behind my lips to begin a dance. To my utter embarrassment, I let out a whimper at the intensity of his kiss. I could feel Fallon's lips curve into a smile before he softly bit my lower lip. Then, kissing his way down my neck, he settled in between my breasts. Rough hands ran over my sensitive skin. Fallon's tongue circled my left nipple until the bud hardened and peaked. He took it into his mouth, causing me to arch my back. I clamped my mouth shut to avoid embarrassing myself further.

"Oh, my sweet Rabbit. I wish you hadn't done that," he whispered. "Hiding your voice from me will just make me want to force it out of you."

"That doesn't sound very nice."

He chuckled. "I'm your villain today, remember? I don't need to be nice."

Large hands gripped my hips and pulled me closer to him. He spread my legs open, kissing my inner thigh. The fireflies in my stomach started their own jazz band as he turned his burning gaze to my core. His eyes traveled back up my body as if drinking it in.

"So beautiful," he purred. Fallon lowered his head to my pussy. The heat of his breath sent tremors of anticipation down my spine. I mentally prepared myself for him to kiss it gently, as he did with my breasts. That I could handle.

No. No, that would be too kind.

My head popped off the bed as I cried out. Fallon went straight for the kill by circling his tongue around my clit before sucking it into his mouth. He groaned as he lapped at the little bud before diving his tongue into my pussy. My legs locked around his head as my arms struggled against their restraints. All the while, my mouth let out some stream of a foreign language I was sure had to be lost in ancient times.

"There's my sweet Rabbit." Fallon lifted his body to peer down at my face. I could feel myself trying to clamp down on the digit he slipped inside me. "Look at me, Cin. That's it, good girl. I want to see your face when I find it."

I bucked my hips against his hold, but he stood firm, holding me in place. The demon grinned as another thick finger pushed past my lips and curled upward, finding—*Oh burning hot ghost peppers*—finding my sweet spot. The pleasure was blinding. It tore through me like the flames he sent down on buildings. I cried out as tears built up in my eyes. It was so much.

"You are making it increasingly difficult not to just mark you now." There was a glint in Fallon's eyes that made some primal part of me want to get up and run—but a much more aroused part of me wanted to beg for more.

His breath came out heavy as he lifted my ass higher to place a pillow underneath. He ran a hand slowly up my body. He dragged his nails so gently, the sensation commanded all of my attention. He teased my breast as his other hand worked my clit.

Fallon seized my throat in a swift motion before forcing two fingers deep into my pussy. His eyes stayed locked on mine as he squeezed my neck. His fingers pistoned their way mercilessly into me. I cried out at the sweet corruption. Any hope of keeping a shred of dignity in this affair went out for milk and never returned.

"Gods, you are a little masochist, aren't you?" A tortured laugh rumbled through him. "The depraved things you make me want to do to you. Foolish Rabbit. You should have run from me. There will be no more chances after this."

Was Rabbit my name? Where was I? I couldn't think past the ecstasy. "Fallon, please!" I cried out, not even sure what I wanted. White-hot pleasure just kept building higher with every thrust of his fingers.

He closed his eyes and tilted his head, long black hair tickling my chest as he groaned. "Yes. Beg me. Say it again."

I cried out as my hips bucked uselessly against his hold.

"Please!" I groaned, drunk off my own pleasure.

The pressure released from my neck. Fallon grabbed my hip before bringing his mouth back down to my clit. I sobbed as he teased the excruciatingly sensitive bud. His tongue flicked at the aching flesh again and again until a whimper escaped my lips. I arched and gasped as his fingers angled up to hit the sweet spot inside me even more. My body shook as he licked me again, following the rhythm set by his hand, and then... My eyes flew open as Fallon sucked hard against my clit. All at once, the pressure that had been building up released in a violent display of shuddering euphoria. My wrists strained against the blanket-bindings as I moaned out his name. He worked me through my orgasm, torturing me with his tongue and fingers until my body convulsed in the afterglow.

I slumped down when he finally pulled away.

"Turn to your side," he murmured.

After a moment of trying to remember how to move, I obeyed. My demon settled himself behind me before I felt something hard against my backside. He lifted my leg up slightly to slide his cock between my inner thighs. I lifted my hips to allow him better access to my pussy. Instead, Fallon closed my legs around his member and began thrusting his cock between my thighs. He moved an arm underneath me to play with my breast, while his other hand toyed with my clit.

"I won't fuck you. Not yet, anyway. But it's not as much fun if only one of us gets to finish, don't you agree?" He angled his hips to slowly drag his cock against my pussy. It was so close. One change in his thrusts, and he'd be inside me. My body burned with the idea of it. With each sure stroke of his cock,

I felt an aching emptiness deep inside me. But he wasn't going to do a damn thing about it unless I told him.

My face heated up with the question on my mind, and I found myself glad he was behind me so he couldn't see it. "Fuck me," I whispered.

Fallon poured kisses on my neck before coming to whisper in my ear. "I will, love. That I promise you."

I groaned as his fingers slid between my pussy lips as he worked his cock faster. "Just not today. I've pushed my luck with you enough."

My retort died in my throat as he slipped a finger inside me, as his free hand squeezed my breast. His teeth grit as he rutted between my thighs in earnest. His powerful strokes nearly sent me off the edge again. I panted and tried to thrust back against him, highlighting that delicious friction. Fallon bit down on my shoulder and growled. Apparently, that was all the invitation my body needed before spiraling out of control. My second orgasm washed through me as Fallon grunted, spilling his release on the sheets.

"Holy shit," I panted.

Fallon let out a laugh and reached up to untie my wrists. They throbbed slightly as blood rushed back into my hands. I dropped them down beside me and snuggled closer to my demon. He laid an arm around my waist, tucking me closer. "Marrying a dragon doesn't seem so bad anymore, does it?"

I giggled into the soft pillow, unable to waste the strength to swat at him. "The council has deliberated. While your arguments are sound and just, we must gather more evidence before a ruling can be reached."

Burying his nose in my hair, he breathed deep. "Madam, this is a kangaroo court," he said ruefully.

"A kangaroo court?"

"You have intentionally ignored evidence that would be in favor of the defendant." His thumb traced delightful circles on my arm, pulling me closer to sleep.

"Evidence like what?" I murmured.

He paused for a moment. "My massive cock?"

A very unladylike snort slipped past me before I burst out in a fit of laughter. Fallon laughed against my shoulder before pulling the throw blanket over us.

# Chapter 10

L ight shone through the bedroom windows, interrupting me from my sleep. With a groan, I snuggled further into the blankets. The sun could go fuck itself. The floor beside the bed creaked. When I opened my eyes to see the cause, a man's face was mere inches away.

"Good morning, sleepyhead," Felix said. I jerked away from him in surprise. The chipper blond laughed and backed away from the bed. He must have taken advantage of the coliseum's washroom, just as we had yesterday. The werewolf looked refreshed and clean. Amazingly, the cuts and bruises I saw on him when we met were all but healed up. His blond hair was even more striking when it wasn't covered in dirt. He'd clean up nicely with a haircut to get it out of his face. Despite the traumatic events of yesterday, Felix's posture was relaxed and carefree, like the man didn't know the meaning of a bad day.

I tried to sit up, but he quickly held a hand up. "You're naked, dear."

"Oh shit," I squeaked, shielding myself with the blanket. "What are you doing here? Where's Fallon?"

Felix walked over to a nightstand by the window and patted on a pile of neatly folded clothes. "I'm here because you two love birds never showed up at the docks yesterday. Although, I'll admit, when I told you to bat your eyes at him to see if that dragon would stop rampaging, I didn't think you'd take it so literally." He wagged his eyebrows, making me hang my head in embarrassment. "Oh, don't pout! It worked. As for your second question, I think Fallon went to go find your horses. I'm to guard you and bring you down to the docks," he said with a mock salute.

"Right, my now-flying horses," I muttered.

I dressed quickly, ready to leave the ruined city as soon as possible. Felix guided me down to the coast, chattering about whatever thought popped into his head. How someone could be so chatty so early in the morning was baffling to me—especially while walking through a ruined city. He had just broken free of a curse, so I realized he just had a lot pent up.

When we approached the bay, we were met with the screeching of an infuriated Usha. The woman was standing on the bowsprit of a large brig. Or I should say, Fallon was standing on the bowsprit of a brig, and Usha was flailing in his arms, screaming obscenities at a man on the dock.

"EVERY HOPEFUL PURE THING IN THIS WORLD TURNS TO ASH IN YOUR HANDS. YOU ARE THE SICK BRINGER OF MY MALCONTENT! THIS IS AN INJUSTICE I HAVEN'T FELT SINCE YOUR COKE HEAD OF A FATHER STOLE MY STABLE LANDS!"

She threw her shoe down at a disheveled man in purple.

"My father bought that land fair and square, you banshee!" Tyrice screamed back at her.

Several demons looked on in amusement from the deck. Then more men simply moved around the screaming pair to load things onto the ship. I noticed with no small delight that four orcs were hauling in copious amounts of alcohol they must have raided from the liquor store. I'd have to befriend those four later. A good glass of wine was just what the doctor ordered.

I ran to the dock before the screeching woman could throw her remaining shoe. "Usha, what is going on?"

Wind whipped Usha's wild blood-red hair around her face. She growled and shook her head to dislodge a curl that had got into her eyes. "Your fucking dragon didn't kill Tyrice like I asked him to!"

"AH-HA!" Tyrice screamed, pointing an accusatory finger at her. "So you admit it! You sent that dragon to burn down The Worthless Gazelle!"

"NO! I ask him to burn down YOU! He thought you'd be in The Worthless Gazelle."

I shot a look at Fallon. He was doing his best to keep Usha and her flailing limbs from knocking them both into the water.

"You let her send you out on an assassination?" I asked.

The demon grunted as he shifted back on the bowsprit toward the ship deck. "When we were riding over to the temple, she asked me if I'd kill him if I saw him during the fight for the chalice. I saw the inn and took my chances."

I rubbed my temples to relieve my growing headache. "What is going on with you two? Was it a nasty breakup or something?"

"What?!" the rival innkeepers shrieked in unison.

Tyrice curled his lip. "First of all, I'm married. Second, even if I wasn't, I could do better than that overweight she-whale."

Felix and I gasped in shock. Usha bared her teeth and looked ready to chew Fallon's arm off to get to the offending man.

Tyrice grinned at her reaction. "If you plan on stealing that ship, you better tell your precious demons to reinforce the deck to hold your fa—"

Before anyone could blink, Ambrose shot out from god-knows-where and slammed his tail into Tyrice. The man went flying back and crashed through a wooden wall into a storage shack.

"Now that's how it's done!" Usha hollered, clapping her hands in delight.

I clapped too. Past grievances aside, the whale comment was too far. The lamia made his way to the loading dock, where Usha happily ran over to throw her arms around him. The things that made that woman happy were...concerning. Though Ambrose didn't seem to mind. Instead, he wrapped an arm around her waist and guided her back onto the ship.

"And so it begins," Felix sighed.

I looked up at him to see him watching the pair with a bored expression. "Oh, you think Ambrose likes Usha? They do seem cozy."

The werewolf shook his head. "Not just Ambrose. Look around them. Every other demon is burning daggers into that snake's back now."

Sure enough, I could spot six men pausing from their loading task to glare at Ambrose. The bear-shifter I met before licked his lips as he stared at Usha. "They're acting like they've never seen a woman before."

"Do you really not know?" Felix's brows drew together as he regarded me like I'd just grown a second head.

"Know what?"

He began walking to the loading deck, beckoning me to follow. "Demon women are few and far between. Life behind Volsog gate is harsh. There's little food to go around, and even if you do survive, you could simply die from the sickness brought on by Myva's curse. It usually affects females a lot worse than men. So they're left weakened or dead by the time it's over."

"That's awful!" My hands fidgeted together as I imagined the horrors these people had to face just because we were tricked into worshiping a false god. The damage done to Wandermere seemed insignificant in the face of what they must have gone through. Though I wasn't happy I had to be the one to come and do it, I was glad we were putting a stop to that evil witch once and for all.

Felix nodded. "Yes. So you can imagine the desperation going through these men's heads now that there are two females aboard this ship. Not only that, the two females responsible for freeing them of their bindings. I doubt any of them are dumb enough to challenge a dragon for you, but that snake is about to have a lot of competition."

"You don't seem all that perturbed."

He grinned and let out a chuckle. "Werewolves bond via imprint. I won't have any desire to chase after a woman until her scent calls to me and tells me she's mine." He turned to give me a wink. "Although that doesn't stop me from having fun until I find her."

"Charming," I drawled. "So, what's intermixing like behind the gate?" The strange makeshift crew around me was full of all different types of demons. If any of them didn't get along, this could be a very awkward boat ride. "Is everyone going to be alright in such close quarters?"

"Probably," the werewolf replied with a shrug. "Don't get me wrong, no one was above killing each other when food got scarce, but I don't think there's any deep hatred between races. As long as we followed the rules, no one felt the need to go to war. Life was too harsh as it was."

"What were the rules?" I asked.

Felix held up a hand to count off. "Don't touch an orc's gold, don't go into a dragon's lair, don't drag a vampire into the sun, and don't taunt the Hungry Man."

I stopped dead in my tracks. "Wait. The Hungry Man?" He ignored me and continued walking up to the ship. "F-Felix wait, the Hungry Man is real?"

He refused to turn back around. But his shoulders shook slightly. He cleared his throat before looking around. "I sure hope one didn't make it onto the ship."

My teeth grit as indignation rose within. "Fallon put you up to this, didn't he? You are both terrible!"

"Well, it looks like my task is complete, Mrs. Dragon. I should probably help the men with loading the deck." With that, Felix dashed off before I could question him.

Above me, my two horses glided onto the ship, their hooves clicking against the wooden deck. Smash came over to greet me while Crash was content to lay himself down next to the railing for a nap. I scratched her chin the way she liked before heading to Usha. The woman had made her way into the captain's quarters and was bent over a map on a large wooden table.

"Are you OK, hun?" I asked Usha.

She paused and looked up from the papers she was rummaging through. Kiki yawned from her spot in a corner. The hyena glanced in my direction but ignored me and rolled on her back for a better nap.

"What, with Tyrice? He got his comeuppance, so it's fine now."

"Well that, and the large number of men on this ship. Felix said they're not used to women. Has anyone harassed you at all? If so, I'm sure we could get Fallon to throw them off."

She laughed and waved a hand in dismissal. "I've lived in the city my whole life. So dealing with a few handsy men is nothing new. And no, no one has come near me. Most likely due to him." She pointed at Ambrose. He stood at the window with his arms folded as he watched the crowd of demons come and go on the ship. Usha tapped my arm and beckoned me closer to whisper in my ear. "He tore a man's arm off this morning. I think that set the rest straight."

"Oh." I thought back to when I had to stop Fallon from doing the same thing back in Boohail. Was tearing off limbs some kind of show of affection for demons? *How over the top.*

Behind us, a giant ogre dressed in gladiator-wear knocked on the door. "Ship's all loaded up with as many goods as we could salvage, Captains. Where are we headed?"

"Captains?" I asked.

"They took it to a vote this morning while you were gone,"

Usha explained. "You smashed the chalice and freed them, and I'm the only one that's been on, let alone steered, a boat, thanks to my father being a sailor, so they made us dual captains."

She shrugged and turned to the ogre at the door. "Tell the men to set sail for Rum Bay."

He nodded and walked away.

"Usha, I don't want to be captain!" I had a hard enough time dealing with one demon. I didn't need an entire crew looking to me for answers.

She rolled her eyes. "So be the quartermaster."

"Great! Yeah, that sounds better." I nodded as relief washed over me. "What's a quartermaster?"

"It means you're second-in-command and in charge of all supplies."

"That's still a leadership position," I whined. "Can't I just be the cook?"

The new captain hung her head and groaned. She pounded her fist on the table and looked me square in the eye. "Cin, hun, I'm going to need you to focus up. This morning I counted one hundred people on this ship. Us included. Three of us are women. I'm not handing control of the ship to a group of horny men. So you will straighten your back, put some bass in your voice, and be the second-in-command. Got it?"

I swallowed. "Got it."

"Good."

"Who's the third woman?"

"She's a centaur named Holly. I showed her how to prepare the ship for sail this morning, so she should be supervising that now."

*Damn, Usha is good at this.*

"So what's at Rum Bay?"

The redhead pointed to a small island in the middle of the Northern Sea, which separated two continents. The lower one was shaped almost like a broken heart. A river came from the Northern Sea and split down the lower landmass until it formed a giant lake near the center. On its right was a drawing of a castle titled Goldcrest City. I wondered if Priscilla was still there. Or if she had met up with the rest of the hero's party and moved on.

At the tail end of the lower continent was Kinnamo, my home country. It spread across the bottom-right side of the heart before splitting off into five separate smaller countries on the northern edge. To the lower east of Kinnamo was another city—Wandermere. Its distance was rather far from the tiny edge of the coast that contained my hometown. To think I'd traveled so far from home was thrilling, even if it made me a little homesick.

"It will take us at least two weeks to reach Rum Bay. However, it's a known pirate bay, so if any followers of Myva come looking for us, they won't risk going there," Usha said.

"Like the hero party," I guessed. If the stories of the last hero party were true, Priscilla and the three other heroes would have the power to destroy whole armies of demons. Of course, I had no way of knowing if that was because those demons were suffering from the ill effects of the goddess' curse or not, but there was no way I wanted to risk the crew's lives in finding out. I decided that if we could avoid them, then we would.

Usha nodded. "We can restock our supplies there and spend time recovering from the trip. It separates our continent from the Northern one containing Volsog gate. The next closest temple will be in Kirkwall." She pointed to another city on the upper west coast of the broken heart. "After we hit that one, all that's left is to double back and hit the one on the Northern continent. No one lives there because it is close to Volsog gate, but the area is covered in icy mountains. So the ship will only take us to its shore. The temple is said to be placed on top of Ubbin's Eye here." She pointed to a large mountain in a sea of smaller ones. They spread across the border of the Northern landmass like a spiked necklace. Beyond them was a drawing of a stone wall that must have been Volsog gate. The structure went from coast to coast. But beyond the wall was...blank— just nothingness.

"OK. I like this plan. What do we do now?" I asked.

Usha stood and stretched. "Well, we just started our new life as pirates. Want to see what liquor the men raided and get fucked up?"

My eyes grew wide at the idea before I nodded slowly. "Yes. Yes, I would like that very much."

The answer to that question was every liquor. The men had raided every brewery and butcher shop they could find. I had never been happier in my entire life.

After Usha was satisfied with our course, she claimed the first order of business of the new crew was to cook a giant feast. It was one that I was more than thrilled to supervise as my first task as quartermaster.

I chose ten orcs to help man the kitchens. They seemed to take direction well and weren't covered in fur like the beast-men. They agreed, on the condition that they got first pick on choice cuts of meat. Seemed fair to me. Although, it did take me a minute to get used to the sight of them eating raw pig hearts. I would have picked the shoulder as the best cut, but to each their own, I suppose. It was funny—a few weeks ago, being so close to not one, but ten orcs would have absolutely terrified me. Yet here I was, showing my new friends Isaak and Baraku how to create the perfect dry rub for roasted pork.

"Captain!" a light green orc cried. "Tell Balabash not to hog all the intestines! He had his fill already!"

He stomped his foot and pointed to the tallest orc, who had a dark rosewood red complexion. Half of his long wavy hair was tied back in a bun, showing off three gold rings in his ears. Each of the orcs had some variation of gold piercings and tattoos, though this one seemed to prefer smaller hoops than the rest.

Balabash turned to me, half hunched over with pork intestines wrapped around a serving fork like giant spaghetti. His nostrils flared as a darker red ran over his cheeks. His eyes guiltily shifted between me and his "spaghetti" and back again, then he swallowed. "Captain, Pasha's being a snitch!"

Pasha's mouth fell open, his nose ring swaying, before flinging his arms at Balabash and looking to me for help. As if he couldn't fathom the crime unfolding in front of him.

I might have laughed if it wasn't one of the grossest things I'd ever seen. "Balabash, please don't hog food."

The accused snorted. "I'm bigger than the rest of these shrimp, so I need bigger PORTIONS!" He accented his last word by slamming a beefy hand on the kitchen counter.

I yelped in surprise and took a step back.

Isaak put a hand on my shoulder and glared at Balabash. I imagine the gesture would have been more comforting if his hand wasn't the size of a bear's paw. While Balabash held the title of tallest, Isaak was the bulkiest orc of my strange kitchen crew. His left tusk sported two hoop rings. They matched the gold bands adorning the long, dark green braids resting past his shoulders. Like most of the orcs, he had a ring of intricate tattoos around his shoulders. They started just below the back of his neck before branching out to his shoulders and coming around to meet at his collarbone. Their style reminded me a lot of my ma's head tattoo.

"Don't shout! You'll scare the poor thing and bring that dragon in here!" he said, also shouting.

His words seemed to break through, and the red orc shoved his bowl of goods into Pasha's eager hands. The smaller orc happily shoved a generous portion into his maw before glancing back at me. He stabbed his fork into more of his prize and held it up to me. "Did you want some? It's fresh!"

Ignoring the twist in my gut, I shook my head. "It's all you, man."

"Suit yourself," he said before digging in.

Isaak and I went back to reapplying the dry rub to the roasting pigs.

I wondered if my ma's tribe had any stories of humans and demons working together like this. Most of them involved noble warriors coming together to fight some kind of big, terrible evil. None ever mentioned the silly things that could happen in between battles. I hoped there were a few that did.

Maybe humans wouldn't be so terrified if they got to see this side of demons. As big and imposing as these orcs were, they acted no different from my brothers and I having a spat. It was enough to make a girl feel a little homesick. But it was nice to have people around again—even if their eating habits were fucking gross.

Once everything was prepared, I kicked open the door to

the kitchen, holding a tray of cheese and fruits, followed by my kitchen orcs and their own trays of food. The crew was spread all about the deck, drinking and stomping their feet to cheer on the coming feast.

I assumed some of them would need to be down below to row the ship, but city folk also apparently used magic on their boats. The oars at the bottom of the vessel moved steadily, even with no one to operate them. The lower deck was filled with cabins to hold a crew with a magic tablet in the center to control the oars' direction.

"Oh, I can't wait to tear into that pork!" said a minotaur, stepping forward.

He was punched in the head by the same lion-shifter I'd met at the coliseum. "Wait your turn, you overgrown bull! Let the ladies eat first!"

The minotaur rubbed his head and growled at his attacker, but took a step back.

Usha hopped up from her chair near the captain's quarters and trotted over, followed by a female centaur who must have been Holly. The centaur walked with a graceful stride. Her long dark hair was braided at the top of her head while the rest fanned out at her back. The horse half of her body was a dark chestnut with a large white patch on her rear.

"Don't have to tell us twice!" she said, grabbing a plate and a cup of mead. I followed her example and piled my plate with all the goodies I felt I could stomach before following her and

Usha back to their small, round table. When we settled in, I noticed the men were still not going near the food. Instead, they kept their eyes on me.

"I want to hear from Lichbane!" Felix shouted. Like an asshole...Lichbane sounded cool, though.

"Chainbreaker! Chainbreaker!" another man hollered.

Soon the deck erupted in a chorus of stomping feet.

I looked at Usha for help, but she shrugged. "It's all you, hun."

*This is my nightmare.*

When I gazed at the crowd of faces looking at me, a sense of calm settled over. I didn't want to or try to be aboard that ship, but I was. If I had turned tail and run away, those good people would still be in chains. More people would be out of their minds with a fatal sickness the false goddess caused. I was tired, and I was hungry, and I was having weird skirt feelings about a man I probably shouldn't be having weird skirt feelings over—but abandoning the quest halfway through was not an option. So I chose to go all in. I took a deep breath before raising my voice.

"In the past few weeks, I left the only home I've ever known, abandoned my religion, and picked a fight with a false god. None of that compares to what you all had to face for the past few hundred years at her hand. So she thinks she has the right to control everyone in this world? Well, I say we have a right to put that lich's head on a fucking pike!"

The men roared at the thought of Myva's blood in their claws.

"Raise a glass to a new era!" I yelled, holding my mug high.

The men stood and followed suit.

"One where we're free of Myva's tyranny!"

Demons of every shape and size celebrated and dug into the feast before them.

I sat down at the table to dig into my plate when Usha clapped a hand on my back. "Good work, Cin."

I nodded at her in thanks.

Holly sipped from her mug elegantly before setting it down on the table. "Now that's out of the way... Usha tells me you've fucked a dragon?"

I choked on my bite of pork.

Usha laughed and leaned back in her seat. "Really, Holly? That's the first thing you say to her?"

The brunette took another sip of her wine. "We centaurs are a direct race."

"We can see that," Usha stated before turning to me. "So? How was he?"

My head fell in my hands. "Oh, my filé powder. We didn't have sex, OK?"

My companions exchanged strange looks. "Why not?"

"Yeah, why not?" Felix asked, coming to sit down.

Holly glared at the intruder. "Get out of here, wolf. This is a ladies' chat!"

"Well, as Lichbane's first demon friend, I call best-friend privileges, and I want to hear details." He took a swig of the bottle he carried and gently swatted my shoulder with the back of his hand. "Spill."

When I downed my cup, Usha refilled it without a word.

"OK, so, he went down on me in the coliseum."

"I told ya he'd be a giving lover," the captain said to Holly. How long had they been chatting about this?

"Is there a reason you stopped there? Are you a virgin?" Felix asked.

The liquor warmed my body, so I drank a bit more. "Well, no, but Fallon says he's going to make me his wife and mark me, whatever that means."

Holly nodded, like I'd just said something obvious. "Yes, that's how mating works. I doubt you'll find a man stronger than him. So what's the issue?"

"What's the issue?" I asked. "Well, for starters, he's a dragon capable of burning down a city!"

She nodded again. "Yes, he'd make a fine protector."

Usha rolled her eyes and refilled everyone's drinks.

"I feel like what humans and demons find attractive is very different. We don't go out of our way to find a man that could level buildings. Someone that's sweet and brings me gifts is usually what I go for."

"Seems irresponsible to me. A protector is what's best," the centaur replied.

Trying to change the subject, I peered at Holly. "So which man do you like then?"

She giggled and shook her head. "Oh no, dear, I like women. Besides, the only other centaur on board is my brother."

"Do you dislike Fallon?" Felix asked. "Is he mean to you? Can't say I'm too surprised. Dragons are known for being irrationally angry nuisances. I wouldn't be surprised if he didn't know his cock from his sword."

Anger flared in my chest. "Don't say that! Fallon has been nothing but kind to me! I'm not going to sit here and let you insult him!"

Felix narrowed his eyes at my response before grinning. Holly and Usha shared a similar grin.

"Fuck," I sighed. "I walked right into that one." The feelings I'd been trying to push down stockpiled into an ache in my chest. I drank the rest of my cup of mead to try and force it away.

Holly patted me on the back and refilled my cup. "Let it out, girl."

"He's the most beautiful man I've ever seen," I whined into my drink.

Usha threw back her own mug. "I know, hun."

I buried my head in the crook of Holly's shoulder. "And so respectful!"

Felix swiped a piece of ham off my plate and popped it into his mouth. "So you're going to tell him how you feel now, right?"

"What do I even say?" I asked, shoveling potatoes into my mouth.

Usha laughed and rested her head on her fist. "Cin, at this point, I'm positive you could walk up to that man and say the weather is nice, and he'd take it as an excuse to bed you."

Holly piped in. "Just go up to him and say, 'If you were still thinking of being mates, that would be something I may be interested in as well.'"

Usha stabbed her fork in the meat on her plate. "No, that's too passive! Look, just go up to him, grab him by the collar and say, 'You, me, bed, now!'"

The werewolf eyed her for a moment before turning back to me. "OK, maybe something a little less aggressive than that. Tell him that despite the fear and uncertainty of the path you're on, your desire for him burns hotter than the fires of his magic. Tell him you love him and need him. And that you want to care for him for the rest of your days."

My mouth hung open at his words. Next to me, Holly sniffed and rubbed at her eyes. "That was beautiful."

Usha nodded frantically. "Yeah, go with that one!"

I took another swig of my mead before slamming my cup on the table. "Right. Brilliant plan. I'm going to go find him!"

The trio nodded in encouragement and sent me off. "Report back when you're done!" Usha called.

"Or better yet, tomorrow after you two have...worked it out!" Holly snickered before receiving a high five from Felix.

On that encouraging note, I set off to the main deck to find my demon.

The floor was full of men happily drinking and stuffing their faces. Two guys in gladiator armor wrestled in the middle of the deck while a small crowd cheered and took bets. No one seemed to be segregated off to their own kind. I realized Felix was right when he said there wasn't really bad blood between anyone. It was honestly amazing. Even in my village, certain families couldn't stand the sight of each other. Yet, in front of me, there was a werewolf with his arm slung around a vampire. They cheered and placed bets between a centaur and a minotaur as if they were old friends.

Cherry would have loved this. Stealing a ship with a merry band of demons would have sent my sister over the moon with joy. Pirate stories were always her favorite. A part of me wanted to relax and join them—but all the new faces just made me miss the one I'd come to like the most.

I looked around but saw no sign of Fallon. Taking the stairs to the hold below, I looked through the row of cabins. Finally, in the last cabin on the left, I found my dragon sitting on a bed, staring out the window. An empty plate rested on the bedside table, along with a bottle of wine.

*This was my chance!*

I tried to take a step toward him but found myself rooted to the spot. In the soft glow of the window, he was irrefutably stunning. For the first time in my life, I found myself wanting to touch someone for the joy of knowing all of them. The rays of moonlight danced across his fair skin in time with the ache of my heart. He was so breathtaking. I wanted him to wrap his arms around me so I could forget the rest of the world even existed. *If this image could be forever captured in time, I'd spend the rest of my days in bliss.*

Fallon turned to me and smiled. "Rabbit, did you have fun with the girls? Usha demanded I leave you three to catch up." He glanced to the side. "That woman sure is forceful when she wants to be."

I tried to answer him, tell him I loved him, but the words burned away in my throat.

He noticed my hesitation and furrowed his brow. "Are you alright?" Gold flashed in his dark eyes. "Did one of those men touch you?"

*Gods, how do words work?*

"I...um...no. We're almost out of pheasant! So if you want any, you'll have to go for it now!"

"Oh," he exhaled. "I'm full, thank you."

"OK, great!" My response came out in a half-squeak. Mortified, I turned tail and ran back upstairs.

*You blew it, idiot. You had one job, and the words that came out of your mouth were "We're almost out of pheasant."*

I dropped myself back down at Usha's table and nursed my drink. Holly stroked my back. "That bad?" she asked.

"I choked and asked him if he wanted pheasant."

Felix snorted as I slammed my head on the table. Why was I such a coward? It's not like the man was sending me mixed signals. A few days into our little journey and he told me he'd make me his wife. If I'd learned anything from our time together, it's that Fallon didn't make false promises. So why was I so scared to just tell him how I felt?

Usha placed another jug of mead on the table. "Well, there's no reason you have to confess tonight. It's still a party! Let's drink!"

Usha was right. Nothing was stopping me from trying again tomorrow. Then, for sure, I'd tell Fallon how I felt.

It was the last thing I could remember before blacking out.

# Chapter 11

It felt like an ax was splitting my head in two. I awoke with my head resting against Fallon's broad chest. He gently stroked a hand down my side, breathing peacefully. "Are you finally awake?" he asked.

I groaned and shifted to find something had fallen beside me. I turned to see a giant cheese wheel wrapped in paper, followed by more neatly wrapped packages of cheese laying on my side of the bed. One rectangle of cheddar was bitten into. I looked past Fallon to see his side of the bed was also occupied by various cheeses. "Why is the bed covered in cheese?"

"You don't remember?" Fallon put his arms behind his head and settled back down. "Last night, you demanded we bring you cheese and then stated that you were the cheese queen."

I blinked. "There's no way I did that."

"Really?" he asked with a smirk. "Because I fully remember you tasking several orcs to bring you cheese. Then you sat in the captain's chair, and the words 'I am the cheese queen' definitely came out of your mouth."

My face flushed as I brought my hands to my mouth in horror. "You're lying!"

Fallon just laughed. *Oh gods. He isn't lying, is he?*

Felix opened the door to our cabin and stepped in with an excited look on his face. "Is the Cheese Queen OK with us robbing a cargo ship?"

"I am not the Cheese Queen!"

The blond raised an eyebrow. "Look to your left. Now look to your right. You are the Cheese Queen. Does the Cheese Queen consent to us robbing a cargo ship?"

*Fuck my life.* "Fine! Sure. Do what you want."

"Excellent, I'll tell the crew."

With that, Felix closed the door. The sound of his footsteps as he ran away beat into my aching skull like a drum. Fallon tried to reel in his laughter next to me but failed.

"Fallon, before you go upstairs, just do me one little favor and just...just kill me." My demon broke out into a full laugh at the request. "I don't...I don't want to face the world after this, so just cut my throat open, whatever is the quickest way. Just end it."

"My love, I'd sooner kill everyone on this ship to save you the embarrassment."

"Yes, but you'd still know!" I hissed at him.

His devilish grin made my heart skip a beat. "Yes. I will always know. Now hold still." Fallon placed a hand on my forehead. His warm skin did nothing against my burning headache. Then, before I could shrug him off, his hand glowed with the same black light he used to turn into a dragon. After a moment, my hangover vanished as if it was nothing. My body felt restored entirely, lighter even.

I breathed a sigh of relief. "How did you do that?"

He returned his hands to the back of his head and closed his eyes as he relaxed. "Magic, my love. It has a lot more uses than just rowing a boat or making hot water." He opened one eye to watch me. "Well?"

"Well, what?"

"Shouldn't I get at least fifty points for curing your headache?" His grin was teasing and horribly adorable.

I settled into his side again and wrapped an arm around his waist. He smelled like a bed of roses and home. I don't know when his scent began to make me feel like the world fell away, but it did. It just felt right. He felt right. "How about nine hundred?"

Beneath my ear, I could feel his heart hammer in his chest. "Could you repeat that, Rabbit?"

My cheeks burned as I felt the familiar sting of

embarrassment. But I wouldn't back away this time. I was done with that. "Fallon...I think I love you."

In a blur of motion, I found myself pushed against the cabin wall, trapped between wood and my demon. Fallon's black eyes burned into mine as he searched my face. He ran a frantic hand through his hair. "Cinnamon, don't toy with me. I need you to mean that." He squeezed my hips as if he thought I would run away if he loosened his grip. I suppose a few weeks ago, I would have.

I forced myself to meet his gaze. "I mean it."

His breathing became quicker as the black shadows of his magic formed a light fog in the room. "I haven't changed what I am." The grip on my waist tightened enough to leave the bruise of fingerprints when he let go. "I'm still a demon capable and willing to kill whoever is in my way. I could snap you like a matchstick if I wanted your life." He paused as if to gather himself. "But, Cin, it's not your life I crave. If you agree to this, if you accept me, it's your soul I'm going to take."

My hands trembled as I brought them to hold his face. "Take it," I whispered.

The dark fog seemed to swirl around the room, blocking out anything that wasn't Fallon. But, in the mist, I could see tiny embers of light. They danced like so many stars in the night sky. Fallon's body shuddered before he put his lips on mine.

*Oh no. This was a mistake.*

I thought kissing Fallon might be a sweet affair that turned heavy as our desire grew. The way you see it in kissing books, all soft lips, and declarations of love. But this demon wasn't exaggerating in the warning he gave me. This felt as though he had opened up my soul, tasting, feeling, and seeing every dark part of me I wasn't used to sharing. His own filled me, almost suffocating in its demands. It was almost like catching rapture in a bottle, its euphoric softness, a kind of aching desperation to feel it again. Like nothing in the world existed but you and this other person. I had the feeling of levitating off the ground and floating in the air.

Oh wait, I was.

Fallon had lifted me to his height so he wouldn't have to bend down, his brawny arms helped him hold my body against the wall.

"Don't fight me," he whispered. "Just submit to it." He placed a soft kiss on my lips once more before skimming his lips along my neck. "Wrap your legs around my waist. Yes, good girl."

I cried out as he bit into my neck. His magic seeped into me with the force of a tsunami. I couldn't move, couldn't breathe. I lashed out with the impulse to escape the frightening invasion, but my limbs weren't controlled by me anymore. The more my body tightened, the more aggressive the magic became.

"Make it stop!"

But Fallon merely chuckled as he soothed me with his mouth and hands. "Just let go. I'm here. It won't harm you. Soon it will feel like an extension of yourself." His brilliant eyes filled with hunger as he bent to kiss me. Against my nature, I forced my body to relax. I welcomed his tongue with an eagerness of my own. I slid my arms around his shoulders as we deepened the kiss. Finally, the magic flowing through me began to feel natural. No longer insistent in its force, but a calming wave flowing through the blood in my veins. It actually felt nice.

I pulled away from the kiss to lean my head back against the wall. My hand ran through his long, black hair as I caught my breath. "Well, that was more in-depth than I thought it would be."

The shape of Fallon's mouth curved into a smile against my throat. "You think it's over?"

"What do you mean?"

As soon as the words left my mouth, an inescapable hunger coiled in the pit of my lower stomach. My clothes suddenly felt too itchy against my skin. I wanted them off, and Fallon's hands on me everywhere. "Oh my god."

"Mmm-hmm."

"Fallon, take your pants off," I ordered, frantically trying to tear off my blouse. The boat shifted harshly to the side, and we both went tumbling to the floor. Above deck, I could hear the excited shouts of the crew.

"Sounds like they just rammed the enemy ship," Fallon said

nonchalantly, next to me on the floor. How come he wasn't as frantic as I was? I was damn near foaming at the mouth, and this man was acting like we were discussing Sunday brunch. It didn't matter. I shimmied my skirt off before reaching for the buttons on his pants. My demon grabbed my hands. "Eager little thing." He grinned, then nodded to the door. "Don't you think I should go help them?"

Help them? My body was on fire, and he...he who burned down a city had the audacity to think of others at that moment? All other parts of my brain that were not connected to my pussy seemed to shut down. "Let them drown. I need your cock, dammit!"

Fallon threw back his head and laughed. A deep booming amusement I don't think I'd ever heard from him. It filled me with a sense of joy that was almost enough to forget about the aching need between my legs. Almost.

"OK, but for real, can we just bang out a quickie before we go upstairs? I've never been this horny in my life. I do not have the faculties to deal with this."

He hummed and sat up. "I know, Rabbit. This is what I've had to deal with since I kissed you in the river."

That man had no right to look so beautiful and so evil at the same time. He leaned down and kissed my forehead.

"Unfortunately for you, we dragons are a little petty."

"What are you saying?" I asked, still trying to free my hands so they could free his dick.

"I'm saying you're going to have to wait a while longer. I can't very well abandon the crew to fight alone now, can I?"

With that, he got up and walked out the door.

I blinked, stunned. *How dare he?*

"You...you did this on purpose!" I roared after him.

His sinister laugh could be heard down the hall. "I love you too," he called back.

It took a moment to stomp down my raging need for dick before I could join the rest of the crew. I grabbed my bow and quiver and rushed up the stairs.

Instead of a full-on battle, I was met with an absurdly calm situation. Our boat was tied off to a cargo ship of similar size. The men of the crew were hauling boxes from the captured ship back over to ours. No one was screaming or running around. Most of them seemed bored if nothing else. I peered over to the captured deck to see a row of men lined up on the side of the boat with their hands up.

Usha shouted orders to the crew of what to take and where to put it, while Holly and Ambrose stood guard beside her. I walked up to Holly, sheathing the arrow I had plucked out.

"What happened?"

Holly glanced down at me and shrugged. "The plan was to attack. But Captain Usha just told them to surrender, and they did. I'm guessing they saw a ship full of demons and decided it wasn't worth the trouble."

*Yeah, that makes sense, I guess. Boring, though. Wait no. Why would I want a fight? I've been on this quest for too long.*

Across the captured ship, I noticed a tall man stagger his way onto the deck. He towered over the humans who had surrendered. I didn't recognize him as one of our demons, but I'd never seen someone Fallon's size that was human. The enemy captain glanced at the stumbling man, but quickly looked away. I recognized Isaak and Baraku, who slowly approached the man. The stranger's long silver hair was half matted to his head. After squinting for a moment, I realized he had a horn hidden in his hair. I ran to the side of the ship and drew an arrow.

"Get away from him now!" I ordered.

Baraku rolled away at my command, but Isaak turned to look back at me. I watched on in horror as the previously shambling man struck Isaak dead in the chest. Blood spurted from long claw gashes as the orc flew back and hit the foremast of the ship, snapping it in half.

"It's a trap; return to the ship!" I screamed.

I lost sight of the human crew on the captured ship as silver mist rolled out from the deranged man like storm clouds. I already knew what kind of nightmare came out of that mist.

Weaving through my own crew as fast as I could, I dove into the kitchen area to snatch up my satchel and fill it with as many bottles of cinnamon as it could hold. I took a sack of the spice and dumped it all over three kitchen rags. I tied pieces of them around my arrows before storming back to the deck.

I should have known Myva would strike back like this. We were so concerned about getting to the next chalice and avoiding the hero's party that I didn't even consider this kind of counterattack. Thunder boomed outside as the sound of chaos enveloped the ship.

When I emerged back on the deck, the men ran around to find every weapon they could use against the dragon. A long silver tail crashed into the side of the ship, sending me and several demons to the ground. At the helm, Usha was turning the steering wheel of our vessel with all her might. Ambrose held her to the ship while his snake half was wrapped around a mast.

"Turn, you hunk of junk!" she screamed.

Scrambling to my feet, I whistled for either of my horses, but the sound was lost over the boom of Fallon's familiar roar. The black dragon slammed into the silver menace until they both disappeared in the blinding storm. I tried again, this time my whistle pierced the madness around me. The fog was so thick it was hard to see my hand in front of my face.

Lightning crackled around me as thunder crashed again. Smash reared up in front of me, nearly taking my head off with her large hoofs. My mare was obviously frazzled but held still long enough for me to clamber onto her back. There was no time to find her reins or saddle, not that I was sure it would even fit around her new wings. Instead, I grabbed hold of her mane and squeezed my eyes shut.

"Go!"

Air rushed past my face as the shire horse sprang into the air. The beat of her wings sounded heavy against the wet fog, and when I opened my eyes, I was still blinded by the storm.

Smash screeched as the face of the silver dragon passed by us in the mist. Black sludge seemed to cover its eyes and bled down the length of its face. The creature roared before lashing out at something in the fog. Hot blood splattered on Smash's side as a horrible screech reached my ears. *Oh gods. He slashed Fallon.* Panic rose in my chest at the thought of him hurt. Or worse, if he was as blind in this storm as I was, he was as good as dead.

I strung up my first cinnamon-coated arrow and fired indiscriminately at the silver dragon's giant body. Two managed to stick around his neck, but three more just bounced harmlessly off the dragon's scales. The beast still thrashed about, seeming unfazed by my assault. *That doesn't make any sense. Cinnamon has never failed before!*

Smash veered right to avoid a collision as Fallon slammed into the storm dragon. His teeth sank into the other's shoulder as they tumbled toward the sea below. As the silver dragon's head passed beneath me, I noticed something brown tied into its matted hair.

*Are you fucking kidding me? Did Myva tie one of her remaining chalices into the dragon's hair?! It would explain why getting shot with cinnamon arrows does nothing. All I have to do is smack Fallon in the face with it for the curse to be lifted off him. That brat of a witch is such a pain in the ass!*

The two dragons skirted the water before shifting back higher into the air—each swirling around one another in a mass of teeth and claws.

Farther into the fog, I could still hear the shouts of the crew as they tried to steer the ship away from the storm. It seemed to get worse the more frantic the silver dragon got. Rough waves slammed into the boats, nearly capsizing them both. The fight had to stop, or the entire crew could meet a watery grave.

"Smash," I called, patting my sweet girl. "This is going to suck so bad." Swallowing my inner coward, I guided the mare above the two fighting monsters.

She let off a stream of neighs that sounded a bit like, "You root-drunk jaguar! What the hell are you doing? Why are we up here?! I want to go home!"

"Me too, girl."

The head of the silver dragon was just below us now. Before I could give myself a chance to back out—or piss myself—I jumped off Smash. My stomach was in my throat as my body dropped helplessly through the air. Fallon let off a terrified shriek as he realized I had slammed into the storm dragon's neck. The silver scales were harsh and cut into my skin as I grabbed his mane to stay on. The long matted hair was like a forest of ropes. Thankfully, that made it easier to keep hold and climb toward his head.

My own dragon gripped his enemy by the jaw in an attempt to stop him from bucking me off. Its colossal body rumbled with the disgruntled roar he let out. The dragon hurled himself forward, trying to dislodge both Fallon and me, but I hunkered down and kept my grip on his mane. My heart dropped as I heard my demon screech as the silver dragon swiped deadly claws down his side. His blood made the air smell of copper and pain. I nearly lost my grip at the sight.

*This isn't how this ends! I'm not losing him right after I agreed to chase happiness with him. I know not all of my favorite adventure books ended happily for the heroes, and I know we weren't exactly the best heroes in this story, what with burning down a city and all. But please, if there were real gods or anyone writing this story, could you make a happy ending, please? We just...I can't take the thought of anything else. I'm not strong enough.*

Inching my way forward, I grabbed the hammer from my satchel and used the claw end to dig further into the hair. My muscles ached with the force of trying to climb up a freaking dragon, but I could complain about that later if I wasn't dead.

Once I got to the crown of the dragon's head, I could see Myva's chalice wrapped in a nest of hair. The familiar sludge was bubbling out of its cup, coating half the beast's head.

Beside the cup was a large festering lump that was nothing

more than a mouth and an eye. "YOU STUPID GIRL! I'LL KILL YOU!" The sound of her voice filled me with more hate than I knew I was capable of feeling. I wanted her dead more than I wanted breath in my lungs. If it wasn't for her, none of this suffering would have come to pass. Fallon wouldn't be hurt, and Usha and the others wouldn't be fighting for their lives.

I grunted and slammed the hammer straight into its eye. "I will take everything from you, you damn lich!"

Myva hollered more colorful words that honestly had no business coming out of anyone's mouth—let alone someone who tried to pretend to be a god. Ignoring her, I slammed my hammer down on the cup over and over, smashing it to bits. The disgusting sludge vanished from the dragon in a puff of smoke.

The giant beast groaned as his eyes cleared. He ceased his attempts to disembowel Fallon. "Thank you," he sighed.

"No problem." I collapsed into the sea of hair. Sweet chili peppers. My body was not built for this.

Before I could relax fully, the silver dragon plummeted out of the air. My hands dug into the ropy hair as I screamed, "Wake up! Wake up!"

The dragon shuddered underneath me as he righted himself. Or tried too. His body shifted and bobbed around as he tried to fly straight.

"So tired," he groaned.

"Cool, but be tired on land, man!"

He tilted his long body downward as my life flashed before my eyes. "Island...hold on." Not that I had any choice in the matter. My eyes shut as I prepared for the worst. I could feel him shift up slightly before crashing into the sandy ground. I flipped upside down but just barely managed to hold my grip before he slid to a stop. The dragon burst into a gray mist, and soon I found myself on the ground. I coughed and spit sand from my mouth. Beside me was the silver-haired man, completely knocked out.

Fallon crash-landed soon after. Black mist enveloped his long body before his human form emerged. He stumbled over to me. I got up and ran to him, and frantically tried checking his side to see how deep the cuts were. Instead, he crushed me against his chest so hard it was difficult to breathe for a moment. "Did he hurt you?"

"Don't worry about me!" I snapped. "How deep did he cut you? Let me see!" I tried pushing him away to get a better look.

My demon let out a shaky laugh and released me. "Careful, Cin, you're showing affection again."

I ignored his teasing to check over his sides. The gashes seemed to close up on their own. I watched, fascinated as the skin shifted back together, as what should have been deep scars faded into angry pink lines.

"I'll heal fine. But I'm so tired."

With that, Fallon dropped to his knees and fainted. I caught him before he could face plant into the sand, and gently guided him to the ground next to the other dragon. When the last of his gashes closed up, I burst into tears. My body wracked with sobs of relief as I held his head in my lap. *That was so close. Way too fucking close.*

## Chapter 12

The second-to-last cup may have been destroyed, but I had no clue where we were. I scanned the horizon around the island we had crashed on, but saw nothing in the distance. No ships, no land, nothing. Not to mention, both dragons were still out cold. I could only hope that Usha was able to steer the boat to safety.

After no small effort, I convinced Smash to help me drag the two men out of the sand and into a grassy valley with a few trees for shade. The mare was hesitant to go anywhere near the silver-haired dragon, but thankfully the sugar cubes in my satchel were too good to pass up. I had no way of knowing when Fallon or the stranger would wake up, so I did what I could to make a camp on the beach.

Without knowing what lay in the island's forest, I wasn't

too keen on searching for food inland. Instead, I tied my knife to a long stick and speared fish along the beach. The shore was teeming with wildlife, so at the very least, we wouldn't go hungry.

To my ever-changing luck, there was a stream of fresh water that led further inland. Judging by the sound of rushing water, there must have been a waterfall nearby. So long as no more deranged dragons or something showed up, this was a pretty nice place to crash land on, almost like a tropical paradise.

After sticking the fish to roast by a fire, I took a quick bath in the ocean then checked on the two men. Neither had stirred for several hours. They did, however, snore. Loudly. Maybe it had to do with the exhaustion of using their dragon forms. I don't remember Fallon ever sounding like he had a vendetta against my eardrums.

I took a chance to check over the new guy. He didn't seem injured, but he had a long old scar running down his face. I wondered what could have caused it. Every scratch on Fallon healed without a trace.

The new guy's hair was still a hot mess. After grabbing my comb, I did my best to rake through his locks while he slept. A few coconut trees were on the beach, so I cracked open a few to help wet his hair and spread a bit of the coconut meat into it to help with the matting. It couldn't have been very comfortable, and it's not like he asked to be Myva's attack dragon. After a good struggle, most of his hair was free of tangles. After rinsing with fresh water, the silver locks looked decently presentable.

Like Fallon, this dragon-shifter's hair was long enough to reach his midback. Maybe this was another dragon thing. I once heard that in some cultures long hair was a sign of strength. Admittedly, I'd only met two dragons by that point, so it may have been a stretch.

Neither stirred once the fish was done, so I ate alone. Throwing another log on the fire, I sat back against Smash's warm body and bit into the red snapper I had caught before. *Damn, that's good.* With all the craziness the quest had thrown at me, the comfort of good food was more important than I could have ever imagined. I just wished Fallon was awake to enjoy it too. The time we spent bantering around food had become precious. I loved showing him all the different kinds of flavor my world had to offer.

But there was no sense in dwelling on it like our journey was over. Fallon was going to wake up. The initial panic I felt when he dropped on the beach had faded. No dying man snored that loud.

My demon rolled to his side and kicked out a foot. Two more kicks later, his body relaxed, and the snoring resumed. I covered my mouth to quiet the giggle bubbling in my chest.

"What are you, a dog?"

My eyelids grew heavy as the events of the day caught up

with me. Everything was going to be OK. Fallon and I were safe, and Usha had Ambrose and Felix to watch out for her. Whatever happened in the morning would be tomorrow's problem.

Body thoroughly worn out, I lay down next to Smash and took one of Fallon's hands in my own. Soon the crackle of firewood was all it took to have me snoring too.

Birds chirped their symphonies over the sound of rushing water. My mind was still far too muddled with sleep to enjoy the noise, so I buried my head further into the warmth in front of me. *Gods, he smells like a sandy beach and sunlight. He?*

Forcing my tired eyes open, I was greeted by Fallon carrying me through the forest. "You're awake!" I gasped out.

"How very observant." His light teasing brought a smile to my face. It was such a relief.

He carried me through the forest, following the river. Soon we came across a great waterfall surrounded by tall trees and wildflowers. Fallon jumped up higher on the ledge of the waterfall before stopping on a mossy slope.

"This will do," he said, setting me down.

I rubbed the sleepiness out of my eyes so I could take in the beautiful scenery. "Do for what?"

"For blocking out the noises you're about to make."

Fallon dropped to his knees in front of me and tugged my skirt off. I yelped as the cool air hit my bare skin. He ran a hand down my thigh before grabbing me by the hips and dragging me closer to him. "Unless you want our new friend to hear? I have no problem taking you in front of him. So long as he sees you are mine."

I covered my face with my hands. "Fuck." The image of that was way hotter than it needed to be. Fallon pulled my hands away from my face and pinned them to the sides of my head. Tendrils of his long black hair fell gently against my collarbone. His voice dropped to a dangerous whisper against my ear. "What did I tell you about hiding things from me?"

I shuddered as he bit my ear. Finally, my hands were freed as Fallon braced himself on one arm before dragging his knuckles against my neck. Hooded obsidian eyes pulled the rest of my mind out of slumber. "Are you going to be good? Or am I going to have to tie you up again?"

*Oh lord, the choices.* Just like before on the ship, my hunger for him was beyond desperate; it was savage. I'd always considered myself a proud woman. But if he pulled away now, even for a moment, I'd resort to begging. "I'll be good."

Fallon smiled at me with a look of such tender devotion that my chest felt tight. He drew me to him, capturing my lips in a kiss. This time there was no gentleness. My lips parted, giving in to his tongue's commanding demand for access. He brought his hand to cup the side of my face as he drove his tongue into me. My body came alive at the ferocity of his kiss.

As if the world would bring about the end of days if he ever stopped touching me.

I squeezed my thighs around his hips and buried my hands in his thick hair. He bit my lower lip before diving his mouth back onto mine. The greedy eagerness of his hands struggling with my shirt reflected my own desperate desire to surrender to him. He may have no longer been affected by Myva's curse, but I felt the feral beast just below the surface. My dragon fumbled with the laces before he growled and simply tore it in two. My nipples scraped against his bare chest as my tits burst out to greet the day.

When he pulled away, I was left panting. The cool moss on the ground cushioned my back as my demon poured lavish kisses on my breasts. I moaned as he worshiped each one.

He circled his tongue around my sensitive nipples while caressing them in his rough palms, working them until they were tight little buds in his hands. I cried out as he took a nipple into his mouth. *Oh sweet filé powder.* The way his fangs traced around the softness of my tits was sweet torture. The sensation had me reeling as he ran his tongue down my body. My legs spread wide as that delicious mouth came to be a mere whisper away from my core.

My demon grinned as he ran a finger up the folds of my pussy. It came back slick as my hips jerked in anticipation.

"Look at you. So desperate for me. I've barely touched you, and your body is begging." Fallon let out an almost animalistic grunt as he pushed a finger back inside. Goosebumps raced across my skin in anticipation.

"So don't keep me waiting," I whispered. It was hard to focus on anything other than all the places his body was touching me. Small wildfires of sensation followed his kisses.

Fallon let out a shaky breath as he watched me with hunger in his eyes. "Oh, but I want to. I want you corrupted, on your knees, begging for it. If only so you'd get more of a taste of what it was like to be anywhere near you." I was panting in need as he pushed two fingers inside me. "I want you to know how desperate I was. Having this sweet cunt so close. Doing everything I could not to just grab you and fuck you till I was the only thought that crossed your mind."

My eyes went wide as he curved his long fingers into my sweet spot.

"Oh gods!" I sobbed. "Oh fuck, please!"

"Yes," he growled, as he watched me cling to him. "I'm going to ruin you, little Rabbit." The brutal pace of his fingers had me trembling as I tried to spread my legs further. Anything to take more of him in. Fallon's tongue swirled around my clit, making me see stars.

Tears gathered in the corners of my eyes as my orgasm built rapidly inside me. "Please don't stop!" I begged. He groaned against the sensitive bud and licked me.

"Say it again."

So damn sadistic. But I was going to burst out of my skin if I didn't come soon. "Please!" I wailed.

"Again."

"Fallon, please!" I was frantic. My hands took hold of his horns as I tried to grind my pussy further into his face.

"Gods, you taste so sweet."

Briefly, I wondered if Fallon was an incubus instead of a dragon, because when he sucked on my clit, there was a damn good chance my soul went with it. That, or I was dead. No earthly pleasures were meant to feel this good.

Fallon hungrily tasted my pussy, shoving his tongue deep inside, circling, before pulling out to suck on my clit. His fingers curved up into my sweet spot until I was damn sure the other dragon shifter could hear me screaming over the waterfall. My knuckles went white from squeezing his horns. My back arched as the first orgasm ripped through me like a mobster collecting a debt.

I moaned as Fallon continued to stroke deep inside me, a second orgasm well on its way.

"On your hands and knees," he ordered.

Desperate to chase that second high, I obeyed.

Fallon ran a hand against the curvature of my ass before shedding his pants. The thick muscles of his thighs nudged my legs further apart. I could feel his girth slide against the folds of my pussy.

*Gods, that thing must feel amazing inside a woman. Or painful. I'm willing to take the chance and find out.*

His firm hand guided my upper back down till I was resting on my forearms, giving him an ample view of my ass. My demon groaned as he traced a hand up my back. His free hand stroked my thigh as he drank in the sight. "You're being such a good little Rabbit."

His hand slid up the nape of my neck before fisting his hand in my hair. I gasped as he pulled my head back to whisper in my ear. "Do you want me to praise you?"

My body quivered; the power he had over me seized my senses like a drug. "Yes!"

With a grunt, he thrust deep inside me. The aggressive intrusion had a tinge of delicious pain as my pussy stretched to accommodate him. The way his thick cock forced me open had me digging my nails into the mossy ground. Pain was... not something I knew I was into. The new revelation was filed away for later as I lifted my ass higher to take more of him.

His voice delivered the most addictive groans of approval. "Such a precious love you are."

Fallon pulled out and shoved his cock back in, using the fist in my hair as a rein. Again, my body came alive with a strange mix of pain and pleasure. It felt so dirty, but oh so good.

"You like it when I'm in control, don't you? Of course you do." He thrust in again, then ground his hips into my sweet spot.

"Fuck yes," I moaned, clutching the ground like it was the only thing tethering me to this plane. My breath became erratic as he set a slow, steady pace. Soon, my body grew accustomed to his size as the dull pain turned into increased pleasure. The hand on my hip tightened as I bucked against him. The slow build was torturous.

*Gods, I need more of him. I will burn this entire island to the fucking ground.*

"What's wrong, love?" he asked. I turned my head to see the devilish grin on Fallon's face. "Feeling at the end of your tether?"

I giggled and thrust my hips against him. "Don't be so petty. I made you wait less than a month!" Though it would be a damn lie if I said I disliked this side of him. To see such a refined beauty like Fallon, reduced to a lustful beast over me of all people, filled me with a strange sense of power.

"Yes," he sighed. "But I've loved you since day one."

My heart fluttered in my chest at the surprise confession. "I suppose I'll just have to make up for the lost time."

He pushed my head down against the ground. He grabbed my hip with his free hand as he slammed balls deep into my pussy. My head spun with the force of the orgasm quaking through me. Fallon rutted into me as I screamed out. The thrust of his hips sent a wicked orchestra of pleasure through my body. The sound of his grunts as he took me for all I was worth; a beautiful prayer.

*I could die from this. They'll have to write "fucked into oblivion" on my tombstone.*

*But glory, glory, what a hell of a way to die.*

"Fallon, please don't stop!" Why did I ever fight this? He was right. So much time wasted when I could have had this jaw-dropping demon fucking me within an inch of my life the entire trip. So dumb.

"Be careful what you tell me, greedy little thing." Fallon hooked one arm around my waist and another around my shoulders. He hoisted me up until he was standing. Gravity brought me back down on his cock, making my mind white out with pleasure.

"Oooooh," I groaned out. This new position took my tether from the ground. The only thing I could do was cling to my demon. The hedonistic feeling of being trapped open for him, with nothing else to do but surrender to his will, as he drove me to the brink of madness.

Fallon kissed my neck before thrusting upward. The scream that tore from my throat was probably enough to shatter the last chalice. Across from us, I could see our outlines reflected in the waterfall. My feet dangled helplessly beneath me as Fallon made good on his promise to bring me to ruin. Nothing could compare to it, and I never wanted it to stop.

So I did nothing but give in to the bone-deep ecstasy he was so hell-bent on delivering. My toes curled, and I clawed at the arms holding me up as he continued to bounce me up and down on his dick. Soon my eyes rolled back into my head as my inner walls contracted around him. I came apart with every thrust of his hips, boneless and panting as I choked on the overwhelming ecstasy.

"That's right, squeeze my cock just like that. Good girl. Fuck, you feel so good."

A keening sound ripped out my throat as he bucked into me. His hard body tightened before he grunted and emptied his cock inside my pussy. Fallon ground into me in slow thrusts before lowering us to the ground, tucking me against him. My limbs felt utterly useless as my body spasmed with the after-waves of pleasure. He sighed in contentment as he stroked my hair out of my face.

He kissed my cheek, and I cuddled in closer. Sleep clouded my mind. "Don't get too comfortable, love," he whispered in my ear. "I've still got a lot of catching up to do."

"How quick do demons get hitched?" I asked, exasperated. "Do you just see each other across the room and know, like some fated mate type shit?"

"Yes," he answered simply.

My cheeks flushed. "Wait, what?"

Fallon traced his thumb down my thigh. The warmth of his body was a pleasant comfort against the soft chill of the morning. "It works differently based on the species. Werewolves imprint instantly. Centaurs usually mate with the strongest of the herd, while dragons can scent out our mates. That's not to say there's no choice in the matter. You weren't technically mine until you took my magic, but I knew you were mine as soon as you freed me from the curse." He ran his tongue over the bite mark he gave me before. "But now you have, and there's no escape from me."

My mind raced back to the first temple we destroyed. Fallon had flung his arm around me and had been using any excuse to touch ever since. From scaring me to sleeping next to him in the bayou to practically pulling me into his lap every time we rode in the carriage. Jumping jaguars, it was so obvious. "Why didn't you just tell me?"

He chuckled and pulled me closer. "You were a human, terrified of demons. If I came on like a buck in heat, would it have helped?"

"Um. Yeah." It would have put the thought of him getting bored with me to bed, at least. Wiggling closer into his warmth, a sense of peace took over me. My big, sexy demon wasn't going anywhere. I'd get to feel his love for the rest of my days.

"Please tell me you're joking." Fallon removed his hand from my thigh to pinch at the bridge of his nose.

"No? I mean, I probably wouldn't have jumped on your dick right away. I like to think I would have held out a few days at least." Though I probably would have let him fuck me outside of Wandermere.

His laugh was breathless, bordering on hysterical. "A few

days." Growling in frustration, Fallon sat up. "Get up," he commanded, smacking my ass.

I groaned and rolled onto my belly. "For what? I'm tired," I whined. Fallon pulled me up and wrapped my legs around his waist. I rested my arms against his muscular shoulders as he kissed my neck. "What about breakfast?"

"You can have breakfast after I've had you bent over that boulder," he said, nodding to a rock formation on the waterfall. "Perhaps in the water first, too. How long can you hold your breath?"

"You've lost your mind if you think I'm fucking you underwater."

"Pity," he murmured against my neck.

Grumbling noises rumbled from my stomach. Fallon stopped his ministrations and rested his chin on my head. "Fine. I'll feed you first."

"How gracious of you," I replied sardonically.

Fallon sighed and shook his head as if the world was against him. "Oh, the troubles I go through for my wife."

A thrill went up my spine at his words. "Am I really? We don't need to have a ceremony or register with the church?"

"Darling, we burned down the church."

"Oh yeah." No idea how I forgot that.

My demon traced a hand down the side of my face. His solid, masculine features made me hunger for more than just food. Sunlight reflected off his curved horns, their jagged edges adding a dash of danger to his handsomeness. "If you want a ceremony, then we can have one. It's a human custom, so I know little about it."

I got up from his lap and stretched. My muscles felt sore, both from fighting a dragon and fucking another one. "No need. The whole wedding thing always struck me as a waste of time."

"Do humans really register their mates with the church?" Fallon stood as well, grabbing his discarded pants. "What do they do with the information?" My brows scrunched together as I looked back at him. "Uh. I have no clue. I never thought to ask."

Fallon gave me a deadpan stare. "I see now why Myva was able to trick your species into worshiping her."

"Yeah, well, at least we season our food."

I tied the remains of my blouse around my chest and used one strip of it to secure most of my hair back. The curls were thick and warm. As the day grew hotter, the last thing I needed was the hot and heavy blanket of my hair over my shoulders.

"Any other secret dragon mating rituals you want to tell me? I'm not going to start shooting fire out of my hands, am I?"

Fallon paused for a beat and tilted his head to the side. After a moment, he spoke up. "After a few years, I believe."

My mouth dropped open. "Wait, really?"

He nodded slowly, considering. "I don't have any knowledge of other dragons taking a human wife. So I am unsure of how long it will take for you to harness my magic. Usually, it's an equivalent exchange between the two. Though I haven't noticed a decrease in my own strength." He flexed his hand. In an instant, blue flames danced around his palm. "If anything, it's gotten stronger. By all accounts, I should have been asleep for days after fighting that elder dragon."

My body shook with excitement. Immediately, I thrust my hand out in front of me to see if it would ignite. Nothing. Damn. Placing my wrists together, I thrust out again.

Fallon eyed me with wry amusement. "What are you doing?"

"I'm trying to shoot a fireball. What's it look like?"

He snorted and lowered my hands. "Years, woman. Not days."

On our way back down to the beach, we came upon several fruit trees. I grabbed a couple of mangoes hanging low on the branches, while Fallon took a cluster of bananas. I snatched one off his bundle and tore into the yellow treat. Bananas were too tricky to grow in my homeland, so they were usually too expensive to buy at the market. Most of the fruit and berries in this forest were incredibly rare back home, when I stopped to think about it. The ground was littered with berry bushes, and kiwi vines trailed up rock formations in a vigorous takeover. Even the shores were teeming with crabs and shellfish.

My brothers and I would have killed to come here and stuff our faces.

The world went dim as my mind spiraled. Brothers… family…kids…baby. "OH GODS!" I shouted, almost choking on my banana.

My demon jumped, dropping his fruit bounty, and looked around. "What, what is it?"

Panic reared its ugly head as I pressed a hand to my stomach. "You didn't pull out!"

I could not get pregnant. I didn't even think I wanted to be a mom, let alone one that was traveling around with a merry band of pirate demons.

"Dammit, woman, you scared me." Fallon pointed to an M-shaped rune below his belly button. It was only a slightly darker shade of color from his skin. It was almost impossible to notice if you weren't looking for it. "It's fine. I put this on me when I woke up this morning. You won't get pregnant."

Relief washed through me. I closed the distance between us and dropped to my knees, placing a kiss on the rune. "I love magic. So much."

"Rabbit, you're about to get a long demonstration of how it works if you don't get your head away from my cock."

I pulled away from the rune to see the bulge in Fallon's pants. "Oh." My pulse quickened as heat pooled in between my legs, and wouldn't you know it? I suddenly wasn't hungry anymore. Weird how a good dick could tempt you away from life's basic necessities.

Instead of moving away, I stroked him. His breath came out in a delightful hiss. Looking up rewarded me with Fallon in all his glory. He was still shirtless, leaving the valley of his abs free for my viewing pleasure. I reached up to run my tongue over the hard muscles. His masculine scent was like a siren's call, and I was a sailor trapped at sea for way too long. My demon parted his lips as he gazed down at me. I could see the lust clouding over his eyes as I stroked him.

He tilted back his head and tried to stifle a groan. "I thought you said you were hungry?"

His cock strained against his wool pants. So I did what any excellent wife would do and set it free.

*Gods, he's so thick and big, and he smells so good.*

I licked at the delicious V of his hip bones as my hand closed (well, tried to close) around his length. My fingers didn't meet, but if anyone asked, I wasn't complaining. "It's not my fault you filled me with your dragon slut magic."

Fallon's body shook. "Dragon slut magic?" His thick hair fanned down the sides of his head before brushing against my cheek as he bent forward with laughter.

Despite his case of the giggles, his cock twitched beneath my hand. I palmed the tip for a moment before running my hands down its length, increasing the pressure. That caught his attention. "Well, what would you call it, then? Ever since you bit me, I've been thirsting after you like a dying man wants water."

He closed his eyes and gasped as I ran my tongue over the head of his cock. I can't say I've had too much experience with head, but judging by the way his hands came to grip my hair, I'd say it didn't take a genius to figure it out.

Fallon's laugh came out as a half groan. "You're not wrong. I've just never heard it described that way."

The deep bass of his voice made the blood in my veins run hot like molten lava. I moaned my desire around the head of his cock. A few droplets of pre-cum dripped from his crown, and I licked it away. It tasted sweet and masculine and excellent because of course it did. That ridiculous dragon slut magic was just hellbent on me spreading my legs for him at any moment.

My hand moved down my skirt in-between my thighs so I could rub myself as I touched him. He took a fistful of my hair as he watched me. I groaned around him as I stroked my thumb against my clit. "You enjoy watching me, don't you? You kinky dragon."

His answer came in a throaty laugh. "Oh, Rabbit, you have no idea." His smile was almost sinister, and it made my body tremble with excitement. I was so preoccupied with working his cock that I failed to notice the black magic swirling around us. The sun and surroundings disappeared. Fallon pushed my shoulders back, forcing me to let go of his cock. I could feel the mist wrap around the hand on my pussy before pulling that away too.

"Guys, I found 'em!" It took a moment for my mind to process the new voice. Pushing my lust to the corners of my thoughts, I looked over to see Usha clambering her way up the hill to us. Fallon let his head fall to my chest, an irritated growl rolling off him. Our perilous captain had come to rescue us. *Yippee.*

The redhead swiped a leafy branch out of her vision before

grinning widely at us. Realization seemed to dawn for her a moment later as she took in the sight of our entangled bodies. Her eyes widened as she brought up a hand to her mouth. Quickly, she released the branch, letting it fall back over her face before turning back around.

"Never mind. We need to come back later. They're gettin' it done!" she hollered, waving her arms at the crew in the distance.

"They're doing what?" a man shouted.

Usha cupped her hands around her mouth. "I SAID THEY'RE GETTIN' IT DONE!"

"Usha, why?" I moaned under Fallon. My mortification grew as the sound of cheering could be heard in the distance. Her footsteps faded away as she left. My mind spun with every life choice I'd ever made as I wondered what exactly I did to deserve that moment.

Fallon peered off in Usha's direction before turning back to me. "Well, she's gone. Shall we continue?"

My glare met his hopeful face. "You can't be serious?" I asked. The thought of an entire crew of men cheering as I got my guts rearranged was not something I had on my bucket list. If anything, I wanted to crawl into a hole and die.

My demon raised an eyebrow and cocked his head to the side, as if confused. "Yeah, she said they'd leave us alone."

I smacked his shoulder as I shoved him off. "You are such a man!"

# Chapter 13

Felix's shit-eating grin was enough to have me wanting to turn around and run back into the woods. However, Fallon kept a firm hand on my back as he helped guide me safely down the hill, to where our friends waited. On the shore, I could see our ship eased up on the bank. It looked a little battered, and there was a tear in one of the sails, but all things considered, it looked well for a vessel that had survived a dragon attack.

Usha turned to us, only to copy Felix's grin. "Sorry, did we interrupt your honeymoon spot? I have to admit, y'all picked out a nice place to recover."

Fallon scowled at the captain before throwing an arm around my shoulder. "Yes. Yes, you did."

"I hate all of you," I grumbled before grabbing another banana off of the cluster on the ground.

Holly shook her head before coming to stand beside me. "Did you both come out OK? What happened to that other dragon?"

My shoulders relaxed at the excuse to ignore everyone else's teasing. "Fallon and I are fine. The silver dragon was asleep at the campsite, last I checked."

"I'm up now," the man in question said as he walked over to us with a slight limp. There was more color in his face than a few hours earlier, but he still looked rather haggard. Well, as haggard as those stupidly beautiful dragons were capable of looking.

"Are you well enough to be standing? Maybe you should sit back down," I suggested.

He held up a hand at my attempt to steady him. "Thank you, Madam Shadow, but I will manage. There are more important things we need to discuss than my fatigue."

Usha cocked her head to the side. "Madam Shadow, did you get a new nickname while I was gone?"

I shook my head. "Not to my knowledge."

The silver-haired man looked between Fallon and me. A crease forming between his brow. "You are the wife of the Shadow Dragon, right?"

My demon tightened his grip around my shoulders. "She is."

"Then that makes you Madam Shadow," he said, nodding to me.

"There are different types of dragons?" That explained the storm clouds that followed our new friend when he attacked. But I wondered if that gave Fallon any special shadow magic. Aside from what I had felt when he bit me, he mostly seemed to just breathe fire and turn into a dragon.

"Yes," the newcomer began. "Each dragon holds power over a certain element. Though it takes a few hundred years to get the hang of it."

Fallon looked over at the scarred demon. "You're Dante the Storm Dragon, aren't you? I'm shocked Myva could get the better of a full-grown dragon."

"That I am," he said simply.

I sighed and rubbed my temples. "We're going to need to write some kind of monster manual so I can keep all this stuff straight."

Usha took one of the bananas from the cluster Fallon held and took a bite. "In the meantime, why don't we break here for a week or so? We can all get some much-needed rest. After that, we can head out to find the last chalice."

Dante shook his head. "I'm afraid we won't have time for rest. Myva has become unhinged and desperate. She ambushed me in my territory behind Volsog gate. I nearly destroyed her physical form, but it was no use as I had no access to her phylacteries. During captivity, my mind was in too much of a fog to understand everything, but I know that she's in the process of gathering as many demons as she can control to confront you and protect her last heart. The more time we give her, the stronger she will become. We need to strike now, or it will be too late."

Usha and I groaned in annoyance.

"We just can't catch a break," I sighed.

The redhead wrung her hands as she thought. "If her last heart is in the temple near Volsog gate, then it'll take us over two weeks to get there by ship."

Dante's voice took on a determined steel tone as he stared off into the ocean. "Not if I fly there while tugging your ship along. If I'm quick, we can get there in four days."

Felix rubbed his chin as he eyed the storm dragon. "No disrespect, but can you maintain that form for so long?"

"He can," Fallon said firmly. "The storm dragon is over seven hundred years old."

My eyes widened at the silver-haired man who didn't look a day over thirty.

"It won't be easy," Dante sighed. "I'll be as useless to you as a newborn pup once we arrive. But I was a boy when that damn witch began stealing demon children for her dark practices. My brothers, my friends, were all sacrificed in her dark arts. So I will push myself to the limit if it means I can see her dead."

"You can leave the fighting to us." A wicked grin formed on my demon. "I'm looking forward to seeing the last wisp of her soul blow out."

Usha rubbed her eyes in frustration before turning around.

She clapped her hands to get the attention of the men on the beach. "PACK IT UP, BOYS, BACK ON THE SHIP!"

Several demons groaned in response. One even petulantly fell back into the sand in a protest to further movement.

The captain put her hands on her hips and glared at the crowd. "No one said killing a goddess was easy! Chop chop, let's GO!"

After a bit more shouting, Usha was able to get the men to file back onto the boat.

"Oh God, I'm gonna be sick," I groaned out.

The ship lurched back once more as we hit another wave. My body spun as my stomach protested at the constant swaying and rough movements. To his credit, Fallon had been doing his best to hold me still and keep a bucket on hand.

When Dante said we needed to get there as fast as he could, the elder dragon was not fucking around. After tying several chains to his back legs, the storm dragon took off like a bat out of hell towards the Northern continent where the last chalice was located.

It was a minor miracle in itself that the boat was not torn apart against the crashing waves. My only consolation was that I wasn't the only one unable to cope with the thrashing. Six werewolves and all ten of my kitchen orcs remained below deck with me as we collectively vomited our brains out. I'm not sure what it was with orcs and the lack of sea legs, but they struggled a bit before this, and the increased speed only made it infinitely worse.

"Hell's maw, just kill me now!" the orc named Tobin cried. He doubled over as we were once again bounced on a wave.

A gray-haired werewolf I didn't recognize tried to steady himself against the wall. "Just hold on, brother, it's the fourth day. The blasted dragon has to stop at some point."

I couldn't even tell if it was the fourth day. Honestly, it just seemed like an endless abyss of agony and vomit. I thought, maybe, Fallon and I could get some privacy in our quarters once we were back on the ship. That dream flew out the window along with my lunch.

*Figures we'd land on a beautiful deserted island, only to have to give it up after one measly day to enjoy it.*

My hands felt clammy and weak when they clutched Fallon's shirt.

"When this is over, I want to go back to that island. For at least a month. If anyone tries to drag us off on another adventure or tries to get me on a boat, I want you to set them on fire."

My demon stroked my hair as he nodded. "Intruders will catch my flames." There was a good chance I was going to be spoiled rotten a year into our marriage. Since I started showing signs of seasickness, Fallon had waited on me, hand and foot. No matter how ridiculous my demands got, he met them with soothing words and devotion.

"I want to rest on a beautiful island too," said Tobin.

Fallon shot a glance at the orc, who looked ready to spill his breakfast. "Intruders will catch my flames."

Alright, so maybe the soothing only extended to me. "It's a big island, love. I'm sure we could just claim one part of it," I said.

My demon tensed his shoulders and looked down at me. His brow furrowed and his mouth parted in surprise.

*Oh. I guess I never called him "love" before.*

"Fine," he grunted, looking away. "They can have half of it."

My hand found his and squeezed. The warmth he provided was my only comfort during this ship ride from hell. But it was more than that. Now, when I pictured lazy days by the river, I saw Fallon sitting beside me. Teasing me with scary stories as we hunted for crawfish. The image was simple, but I found my chest squeezing at the thought. When the quest was over and Myva was dead, I decided I'd take my time enjoying my days with him.

Outside, a low roar sounded off from Dante.

"There's my signal," Fallon sighed and placed a kiss on my forehead before getting up. My stomach gave another sick flip as the ship tilted again. I buried my head in my hands as Fallon headed up to the main deck. "We must be close," Fallon announced. A few demons groaned in relief as the dragon started to slow. Fallon's duty was to shroud our ship in his shadow magic so we could blend into the night. At least, if everything went as planned.

According to Dante, Myva's temple was directly atop a mountain called Ubbin's Eye. Whatever forces she managed to gather would guard the mountain's entrance near the southern shore. If we could sneak past them and enter through a ravine located on the mountain's west side, the temple would be ours for the taking. I expected a few high-level demons to be guarding the building itself, but if most of her forces were at the base of the mountain, then this was as good a shot as any.

I dragged my sorry hide up with no small effort and coated more of my arrows in cinnamon. Black mist rolled around my ankles as I made my way up to the deck. Usha stood silently at the helm, guiding the ship through the tight ravine the ship had just entered. Dante's dragon form faded into a silver mist, giving way to a collapsed man at the front of the deck. His breathing came out in labored shakes. Holly wordlessly signaled two large men to grab the fallen dragon-shifter and take him below deck.

I took a deep breath; the air coming out as a cloud in front of my face. The world around me was like nothing I'd ever seen before. In the dark of the night, the mountaintop seemed to disappear into the sky itself. A layer of white covered the ground, with tufts of bushes peeking out. The trees were massive, with sharp needles for leaves.

*Why are the leaves sharp? What fresh hell is this place?*

It was so freaking cold. A gust of wind ripped through the ravine, making me shiver. I bit my lip to keep from griping.

The plan hinged on us being as quiet as possible. No way I was going to be the donkey's ass that needed to sneeze in the middle of an echo-inducing chamber.

Holly tapped her hoof twice to my left. I looked over at the centaur to see her eyeing a blob-like form in the water. Tiptoeing over to her side of the ship, I lined my bow up with the shifting creature. Long red tentacles rose from the water with an almost hypnotic grace. They swayed, feeling the air around them like a sensor. The clawed tips almost reached the height of the mainmast. A hand fell softly on the back of my neck as I drew the arrow. Fallon grabbed my wrist and lowered it back down, never taking his eyes off the tentacled beast.

"Do not shoot the kraken," he whispered. "That is the last fight we want right now."

His dark eyes bled away to gold, and the smoke around us grew thicker, rolling off him in thick blankets. Despite the obvious density of his smog, I could still see the kraken clear as day.

Beside me, Holly extended her hands out in front of her. "I can't see a damn thing," she muttered in an annoyed tone. In careful movements, the centaur guided her hand onto the railing to steady herself. Judging by the lack of thrashing tentacles, I guessed the kraken couldn't see us either. *Odd.*

I tugged lightly on Fallon's shirt. "Why can I still see, is something wrong with your magic?"

Fallon cocked his head to the side before moving his hand in front of my face. I followed the movement to prove I could see it just fine. My demon grinned, then bent down and kissed me. "Looks like you're taking to my magic a lot faster than I imagined. You'll be able to see through my fog now. Try not to get carried away and burn the ship down if your fire comes next."

"I promise nothing," I whispered, grinning back at him.

He placed a hand over his mouth to stifle his laughter.

We glided in silence for what seemed like hours. No one dared to make a sound as Usha steered us with Fallon's detailed directions. My dragon stood still as a statue at the front of the bow as he peered through his mist like a spider surveys its web. He would raise a hand left or right as we narrowly avoided rocks and underwater trees.

*When this is over, those two would make a horrifyingly effective raiding party. Not that I have any intention of going near a ship after this.*

Fallon raised a fist, and the boat slowed to a stop. The men around me grabbed their weapons and donned whatever extra clothing we had. The shifters remained weaponless but in their human forms. They'd need opposable thumbs for phase two. Usha nodded to my shadow dragon as the ship came to a complete stop. His mist flowed back to him in a swirling cloud before the familiar crown of midnight horns cut through it.

The dragon coiled his form around the side of the mountain before lowering his neck to the ship. Wasting no time, the men jumped on top of him, grabbing hold of his long mane for purchase. Felix and Ambrose helped Usha up Fallon's dark scales. I boarded last, taking a seat next to Usha, between my demon's horns. No matter how strong our merry band of pirate demons were, they wouldn't be able to withstand the harsh magic coming from Myva's temple. It fell to the captain and I to smash the last chalice.

*No pressure.*

The icy wind blew past my face as the black dragon glided his way up the side of the cliff. A choking noise caught my attention, and I turned around to see Ambrose wrapping the end of his tail around Felix's head. He rolled his eyes when I raised an eyebrow. "He was going to scream," the lamia whispered.

"Felix, why didn't you say you were scared of heights?" I asked.

The captured blond wiggled his head loose from the snake tail to fix me with a panicked glare. His body was still trembling as his eyes filled with unshed tears. "I didn't know," he hissed in a low tone. "I don't make a habit of climbing on giant lizards."

Usha shook my shoulder and pointed in front of us. There, nestled in the mountain's valley, sat a small temple. Rays of moonlight seemed to illuminate it from the rest of the valley. Behind it was what first appeared to be a massive hill that sloped in such a weird way that I had to stare for a few seconds before comprehension hit me.

*Snapping gators, that's not a hill! That's a giant severed head!*

My skin crawled at the sight of the massive head that seemed frozen in time. It was the size of a barn with one short horn poking out the top of its fractured skull. The beast's teeth looked to be filed down into man-sized swords. Oddly enough, that wasn't the bit that made my stomach churn. In the top center of the giant's head was a lone eye, staring blankly at the temple. Ubbin's Eye, I realized. *Very literal with the names around here.*

"Someone is coming out of the temple!" Usha hissed.

We ducked down to avoid suspicion, which Fallon made utterly pointless by shooting a stream of flames down at the structure. The snow on the ground evaporated with a stinging hiss as the fire rolled over the valley. I watched in growing horror as the flames beat uselessly against an invisible barrier.

Below, on the stone steps of the temple, was a tiny woman in a long red cloak. She held her arms up high above her head as a soft yellow pulse emitted from them. Three more people rushed out to the temple steps. Two of them I knew all too well. They were people I'd hoped to never see again.

"Oh, fuck me," I groaned.

# Chapter 14

Usha's eyes widened as she clutched her ax. "Is that the hero's party?"

"Cinnamon?" Priscilla called.

"What?" Glen Dupont stared at me with wide eyes as he grasped a spear. "Cin, Sweets, is that you?"

Usha turned to me with a furrowed brow. "Cin, you know these guys?"

"Unfortunately."

**"Why did he call you Sweets?"** Fallon's voice rumbled through the ground until I was sure everyone on the mountain heard it.

*Gods, this is going to be so awkward. Why in the Cyclops' esophagus did my ex-boyfriend have to be one of Myva's chosen heroes? This is some burnt crust bullshit.*

229

I swiped a hand across my face. "Love, this is Priscilla Wilkinson and Glen Dupont. They're from Boohail, like me. Priscilla, Glen, this is my husband, Fallon."

Fallon landed a safe distance away from the temple and lowered himself enough for our party to land with ease. In the distance, a chorus of screeches and roars echoed through the air. I assumed Myva's mind-controlled demons knew we had arrived.

Holly seemed to mirror my thoughts. "You deal with whatever this is," she said, patting my shoulder. "The men and I will form a blockade around the valley entrance. I don't know what kind of forces Myva gathered, so end this quickly." With a wave of her hand, the rest of our party, excluding Usha and Fallon, ran to the valley entrance.

Glen and Priscilla stared at me wide-eyed, while Fallon… remained in his dragon form, eyes locked on Glen. "**Why did you call her Sweets?**"

"Husband?" Priscilla squealed. She twisted her wheat blond hair as her mind tried to make sense of what was in front of her.

Despite leaving on her journey well over two months ago, the petite woman looked precisely the same as the day she left. Her pink ankle-length dress was accented by a beautiful white cloak. A white sash tied around her waist gave the dual purpose of accenting her slight hips and holding her pink sword in place. I couldn't help but snort at the sight of it. She drove the village blacksmith up a wall over the damn thing, after all.

At least she knew what she liked. Though it made me realize I probably looked like some kind of vagabond, with my over-sized white blouse and green skirt we stole from Wandermere. Though to be honest, the outfit was stained brown by that point. Either way, I was not looking my best.

Glen's face contorted into a sneer.

*Lord of the Swamps, please don't let this idiot—*

"I called her Sweets because she's my woman!"

Rage emanated off Fallon as his glare tried to incinerate Glen on the spot. If it weren't for the red-garbed woman's shield, it probably would have worked.

"EX-girlfriend!" I shouted. Fuming at the stupidity of the man in front of me, I reached into my quiver for an arrow.

It was with no small glee that I came to realize that seeing Glen's face meant absolutely…nothing to me. He had the same boyish good looks I remembered, with mischievous brown eyes and high cheekbones. I used to gush over his soft poet's lips before I realized they spilled nothing but lies. He, like his companions, had completely spotless clothing. As if the four of them had simply walked here for brunch. Glen and the other man also sported fancy, spotless white tunics. Though the other woman wore red, she seemed untouched as well. How was that possible if they'd been fighting back demons for the past two months?

Unless they hadn't. If that girl could make a barrier powerful enough to fend off dragon fire, normal demons must not have stood a chance at injuring them.

Glen took a step forward and grinned, cocking his head slightly in the way he always used to do when he wanted something.

"Don't be like that, Sweets. I only left because I knew I was better than that podunk village. I mean, I was chosen by the goddess as soon as I reached Wandermere!" he said, spreading his arms wide. "Looks like you finally realized it, too. After we banish these demons, how about you and I catch up, gorgeous?"

The heroine in red shot out just in time to block Fallon's fiery blast. My dragon roared in frustration and beat his tail against her force field, but it held firm.

Glen barked out a laugh and patted the woman on the shoulder. "You see? No demon stands a chance against us! Thanks to Myva's blessings, our task of exterminating these vermin has been a piece of cake!"

**"Shoot the one in red,"** Fallon hissed. **"Humans are not affected by that damn lich's magic. Shoot the one in red so I can slaughter that insignificant worm."**

The woman in red flinched and sidestepped behind the other three.

"Enough of this stupid reunion," the second male spoke up. His features were hidden by his massive hood. The best I could make out was that he was rather tall and skinny, like a beanpole that never stopped growing. He held a staff with a glowing red stone at the top. I wasn't sure what kind of attack came out of that, but I hoped my arrows were faster. "That crazy woman is clearly working with demons, so let's just kill her before she can kill Nina!"

Priscilla laughed and swatted him away. "Don't be stupid. Cin must have been tricked."

She turned to me and raised her chin proudly. "Just step aside, Cin, with the power of the goddess on our side, we can take care of your demon problem easily."

*This is getting nowhere fast.* "Look, I don't have much time to explain, so listen closely. Myva is not a goddess. She's an undead witch called a lich, and she's been tricking us into protecting her for hundreds of years. Stand aside so I can break her last chalice. I don't want to hurt any of you, but I will!"

I trained my arrow on the shield heroine.

"**I do,**" my dragon grumbled.

"Shut. Up."

Priscilla scrunched up her nose before breaking out into a laugh. "Um, I don't know what kind of drugs you've been snorting, but you shouldn't make up these ridiculous lies just because the goddess didn't choose you."

"Are you not hearing me? Stand aside, or I start shooting!"

Behind us, Holly roared commands at our crew. Chancing a glance back, I saw them forming a defensive line.

With a piercing screech, a manticore slammed itself into one of our minotaurs. In a flash, Tobin skewered the beast in the head.

I broke out in a cold sweat as more monsters began charging Holly and the others. They crawled over the mountainside in a seemingly endless wave. There was no way our hundred were going to fight them off for long.

"What kind of goddess sends demons to do her dirty work?"

Adrenaline coursed through my veins as my fingers tensed, drawing back the bowstring.

**"Cin, shoot her so I can take care of them!"** Fallon shouted.

Glen trained his spear on Fallon as he prepared to strike. "She's not going to kill her own people, you monster!"

The girl in red remained silent as she raised her hands in the air again, ready to block Fallon's strike. I had no idea who the girl was. She could have had a large family, and she could have donated to all the orphanages. Or she could've been an absolute bitch. "Glen's right. I'm not going to kill my own people," I said.

Priscilla smiled, relief easing from her shoulders—until my arrow hit the girl in red. She went down hard. The surrounding snow soon matched the red of her coat. Her small hands grasped helplessly at the arrow in her gut. Her party members gasped and went to her. A grave mistake.

Fallon shot after the hero's party like lightning. His massive claws slashed out at Glen, ripping his arm clean off.

He screamed and rolled away from the dragon's blood-coated black scales. The other man held up his staff as blue lightning burst out. Fallon stumbled back slightly before slashing his tail at Priscilla, who dodged to avoid having her head taken off.

Usha grabbed my hand and rushed towards the temple. "Now's our chance, let's go!"

Snapping out of my daze, I bolted into the temple, not daring to look back at how Fallon was faring. The faster we broke the damned cup, the safer my people would be.

Usha's and my labored wheezing carried through the marble building. As we passed through the doorway, a horrible stench of death greeted us. My nose burned as bile rose in my throat. My companion coughed into her arm before grabbing hold of her ax with two hands.

"Well...isn't this nice? You've brought a little friend this time," came a foul-toned voice from the center of the temple. I realized it had come from the last chalice.

Muck was bubbling over its rim as sludge and bones took shape on the floor. A hand reached out to snatch the cup off its altar as the mess took the form of a woman who looked like plague incarnate. Her body was riddled with sores, and her skin hung off her bones like grease melting off a frying pan. Her green eyes lay sunken deep into her face, as fingers, more bone than skin, tapped on her last phylactery.

"Myva." My bow notched another arrow.

Usha recoiled at the sight, clutching her ax to her chest

like a lifeline. "That's the goddess? I imagined those stained-glass windows had a bit of artistic flair but—great day in the morning—that's just an outright sham!"

The lich snapped her head to glare at Usha. A clump of gray hair fell from her head and slid down her tattered black dress. "Silence, you ignorant wretch! I am the GOD of you mortals. How dare you spit in the face of my gifts!"

"Gifts? Generations of demons were lost because of your curse!" My jaw clenched in aggravation at the abomination in front of me.

"Exactly!" the monster screeched. "Generations of you precious humans being at the top of the food chain because of my blessings. Without me, you humans are NOTHING! Just worthless mortals slithering in the mud without guidance. You two should bow to me!"

Beside me, Usha shook her head and raised her ax. "Oh, so sorry, dear. Bowing is where I draw the line. Bad knees and all that."

Myva's jaw extended like a snake as she let out a piercing scream. The sludge pool at her feet began to rise, forming tentacles. I released my arrow so fast the string slapped back on my arm. I ignored the pain as the arrow buried itself into Myva's open maw with a squelch. Black blood sprayed out her lips, and the tendrils faltered slightly.

"That's one way to shut her up," Usha giggled.

The false goddess ripped the arrow from her jaw with a

roar, then shot a slimy tentacle in my direction. Usha tackled me to the ground before it could meet its mark. The redhead rolled on her side before jumping to her feet. "Or not." With a mighty swing of her ax, Usha lopped off another tentacle as it shot toward us.

"You filthy brats! My beautiful magic is wasted cleaning up after your mess!"

The false goddess struck out in unhinged madness as she clutched her phylactery to her chest. Her movements were wide and wild as she screeched in rage.

I shot at her chest, clipping the cup slightly. She howled in fury as Usha charged at her. The captain swung her ax at Myva's chest, but the lich caught her wrists with a slimy tentacle before slamming two more into my companion's side. The force of the blow sent Usha flying sideways. She crashed to the floor before rolling back and getting up with a roar. Charging at the lich once more, Usha ducked low to avoid another tentacle before catching Myva in the shoulder with her ax.

I shot off another arrow while she was occupied with Usha. This time it broke off the base of the cup before sinking into Myva's left breast. The false goddess roared in pain before swiping her tentacles forward in my direction. I dove right, barely avoiding being clipped. A tentacle wrapped around my quiver, ripping it off my back along with my arrows before slamming it to the ground. *Crap in a basket.*

Nevertheless, I charged her head-on, snatching my

hammer from my belt and bringing it down against the tentacle wrapped around the remains of the cup.

Even as she screamed in pain, Myva refused to release it before retaliating with a swing of her own. Usha and I flew back at the force of her blow. I landed hard on my ass before my shoulder slammed into a door frame.

Stunned, it took a moment for my eyes to focus. I could see Fallon's dark mist just outside the entrance as he tried to hide his location from the hero's party. He favored his left front leg as he glided away from Priscilla's sword. The staff wielder shot bright, white flashes of magic through the air in an attempt to reveal the dragon's location, but they were swallowed into nothingness by the abyss. Even with an arm missing, Myva's dark power coursed through Glen as he thrust his spear at Fallon's tail—but it was clear he had no idea what he was aiming at.

*That's it!* Forcing myself up, I reached for my demon's mist, willing it to come towards me. The strain of using my new magic was intense, like trying to pull a fish trap stuck in the mud. It resisted harder as I tried to pull it past the door frame, no doubt conflicting with Myva's protective magic. But I persisted, trying desperately to tap into the feeling of power I had when Fallon first gave me his magic. After a moment, it felt like my blood came alive. The mist gave way so quickly that I fell back on my ass. Black fog spilled into the temple, concealing Usha and me.

I looked over to see Usha wrapped in one of Myva's tentacles. She cried out in pain as the lich tried to squeeze the life out of her. I shot over as fast as I could and slammed my hammer down on the slimy appendage. Myva screamed and withdrew back into a corner as Usha caught her breath. Her breath came out in wheezing pants as her ax slipped from her fingers.

"Can you move?" I whispered in her ear.

She winced as she clenched her side. "Yes. But I think my rib is broken."

*Shit. There's no way she can take another hit like that.*

I clamped a hand over her mouth and silently guided her to the entrance. Myva screeched in anger, shooting her tentacles around in every direction, hoping to hit something.

We rounded the corner before I guided her to sit down. "You're just outside the entrance of the temple. Don't move. Don't make a sound." She nodded in understanding before clamping a hand over her mouth to keep from crying out.

I peered back into the temple to see that Myva had stopped her screeching. Instead, she closed her eyes in an attempt to hear my movements. Her slimy appendages swayed through the air like whiskers.

About two paces away lay one of my scattered arrows. *Would she hear the song of the string pulling back as I nock it? If she runs me through before I can even shoot, then blinding her has been entirely pointless.*

My fingers twitched near the hammer at my belt. Not an

ideal throwing weapon. Also, she still had a tentacle wrapped protectively around her precious chalice.

The lich grinned, her yellow teeth sinking into black, rotted gums. "What's wrong, little one? Don't you want to shoot me? Go ahead. I'll eat your heart before you can even pull the string!"

*Yeah, that's the issue, bitch.*

Myva struck out blindly again, hitting nothing but the ground. She growled in frustration before limping further to the center of the temple. "COME OUT, YOU INSOLENT WORM!" She unfurled the tentacle, wrapped it around the chalice, and swayed it back and forth. "This is what you want, isn't it? Come then, child! See how you fare against a GOD!"

*Oh, thank goodness she thinks I'm stupid. This I can use.*

Reaching into my pocket, I pulled out a sugar cube, then chucked it across the room. It hit Usha's fallen ax with a slight tink.

Instantly, Myva fell upon the spot where the ax lay with the ferocity of a wild jungle cat. I snatched the hammer from my belt and threw it as hard as I could at the unguarded chalice. By some miracle, the beautiful hammer met its mark, colliding with the chalice dead on. The last phylactery shattered into a dozen falling fragments.

Myva howled in agony as her body contorted. Her skin began to fall off her bones, hitting the floor with wet slaps. I cried out in disbelief before slamming my hand over my mouth. My stomach dropped as the false goddess turned her shrieking face toward mine. "Don't think you've won, little wretch! I still have this body to kill you!"

In a flash, she shot over a menacing tentacle, aiming to skewer me in the chest. Before the slimy terror could seal my fate, a set of massive claws slammed against it—but the tentacle veered around and sliced me across the shoulder. I cried out at the searing pain and fell back. A second later, the roof was ripped clean off the building. Myva hissed in pain as Fallon's hand trapped her appendage in place.

**"But you don't have your chalice's sealing magic, do you, witch? Let's see how well you fare without it."** The dragon's yellow eyes fixed on me. His nostrils flared at the sight of my shoulder.

"Let go of me, you damn demon!" Myva roared like a woman unhinged, desperately whipping her tentacles at Fallon's dragon form. They beat uselessly against his hard scales as if they were nothing.

He ignored her, instead letting his gaze follow the trail of blood running down my arm. A rumbling noise came from his chest. His massive head snapped back to Myva before he slammed his hand down on her lower torso. Fallon's jaw opened slowly as a gust of mist spilled out of his maw in a frenzy. It billowed around the false goddess, who writhed and screamed as if it burned her.

"What the hell is that thing?" Priscilla shuddered at the

staircase of the temple. She sported a gash on her lower leg, and it seemed to take all of her strength just to hold her small sword in front of her. Glen came up behind her with a makeshift tourniquet on what was left of his arm. He froze in shock at the sight of Myva's rotting body thrashing under Fallon.

My breath came out in ragged pants as I tried not to think about how close that was to my end. "That's your precious goddess."

The two heroes looked on in shock and horror. "That can't be," Priscilla whispered. "I don't understand. The goddess has always protected us from demons!"

Glen took a step back and shook his head in disbelief. His spear fell to the ground at his side as he watched the scene unfold in front of him.

"She's the reason demons went crazy in the first place. I'll explain later. Just help me out of here," I said.

The swordswoman snapped her gaze away from the false goddess to run to my side. Priscilla helped me to my feet before we hobbled out of the temple.

I chanced a glance at Fallon. My demon had Myva pinned to the floor with his jaw open. However, instead of more of his dark mist pouring out, it seemed to return to him. Along with it was deep blackish-purple magic coming out of the lich. She screamed under his claws as her magic was torn from her. Her face drained of all its color as what was left of her skin shriveled up like a raisin. *Gross.*

Outside the temple, I looked to the valley entrance to see Holly helping one orc to his feet. Several new demons were scattered around them, looking dazed and confused. No one appeared to be fighting, so I assumed the curse was lifted when the chalice broke. A weight lifted off my shoulders at the sight of them. Felix caught my eye and waved back at me, smiling. He was in his full werewolf form, so the smile looked rather menacing, with his mouth full of razor-sharp fangs. But I was so happy to see him alright, it just made me laugh.

We reached the bottom of the steps near where the staff wielder knelt at the shield heroine's side, wrapping bandages around her torso. Upon seeing me, his face contorted into a sneer as he reached for his weapon. "Priscilla, what the hell are you doing with her?"

"She was telling the truth, Pierce. The goddess is some kind of undead witch!" She pointed back into the temple. "Go see for yourself. These guys are not our enemy."

The hooded man scoffed and gripped his staff. "Bullshit! She shot Nina! If you won't kill her, then I will."

Priscilla cursed under her breath, then gripped the hilt of her sword. But when Pierce thrust his staff in my direction, nothing happened. He blinked at his staff before trying again. Still nothing.

A relieved sigh escaped my lips. "Looks like your gifts are all used up."

He snarled and threw his staff into the snow. Drawing a knife from his cloak, Pierce charged forward. The man was lanky and unstable in the slippery snow. He righted himself as he slipped on an ice patch before dashing forward again.

"Pierce, stop! There's no need for this," the blond woman let go of me to draw her sword. A very heroic gesture, but a man with no magic falling all over himself posed little threat to me.

Digging into my skirt pocket, I took out an apple and chucked it at the charging man's head. It caught him right between the eyes, making his head snap back before his legs slipped out from under him. He crashed to the ground with an embarrassing thud.

"We'll get your friend some help. Just cool off for a bit," I said. I knew I should probably have been a little more sympathetic to the situation, but in reality, these "heroes" had just tried to kill Fallon and my friends. Shooting one in the gut seemed like fair play.

The staff hero didn't seem to agree with me. He rolled to his feet before gripping his knife again. I pulled out another apple. "We can do this all day," I taunted, holding up the fruit. In truth, we could do this for another two apples. My pockets weren't endless.

Pierce opened his mouth to say something, but I blinked, and his head was gone. Actually, his whole top half vanished. Priscilla screamed, and her comrade's blood sprayed onto the cold ground. I braced myself, ready for another surprise assault from Myva. But it was my dragon looming above us. The edges of his obsidian tail dripped scarlet.

My breath caught at the sight of him. Dark horns gleamed in the moonlight like a crown of shadowed twilight. His long body dipped and weaved around the area until it was hard to differentiate him from the mountain peaks themselves. The mist dancing around his feet now contained wisps of purple. They crackled inside the black clouds as if trying to get away. The dragon's golden eyes caught mine. And I know it sounds cheesy, but I felt I had lived a thousand lifetimes in them. Surrounded and protected by that warm gold. *He will always protect me. I know that now.* It was as if he stitched the fact into my very soul. The spell of his gaze was broken when he turned to bare his fangs at Glen and Priscilla. Embers flickered around his maw as he inhaled. Shock coursed through my body as I flung myself in front of the heroes.

"Fallon, no!" I screamed, spreading my arms out to shield them behind me.

My love shut his mouth. The embers fell harmlessly onto the ground. **"Rabbit. Move."**

I shook my head. "I won't." Glen crouched lower behind me. The tremors of terror showed through in the hand he placed on my shoulder. I could feel the rage come off Fallon in the frantic movements in his fog. He roared at Glen with absolute hatred. The human man only shrank down further, unsure of what to do.

"Get away from him!" Fallon ordered.

Remaining still as oak, I tried to make my voice as soft and calm as possible. "I won't let you kill them."

The dragon growled his frustration. **"They are the enemy! They're going to hurt you!"**

"No, they won't. It's over, Fallon. There's no reason to kill anyone else."

**"The one I cut down tried to stab you!"**

"Yeah, and he was terrible at it. Now he's dead. So calm down, and I'll step away from them."

He snorted, the fur along his back standing on ends. **"Calm down, she says."** His head dipped to the left before he paused and swayed to the right, looking for an opening. Fallon let out a frustrated roar before charging. Priscilla shrieked and covered her head. Glen fell to the ground next to her.

I stepped forward.

Large claws closed around my body, and Fallon spirited me away. I shivered as the frosty night air beat against us as we rose higher. My demon's magic rolled over me in a blanket of warmth. **"Sleep,"** the dragon rumbled.

I did.

# Chapter 15

My mouth watered as the smell of good food drew me out of slumber. I wiggled my toes and stretched. My joints gave a satisfying pop. Plush fur blankets lined the large bed I was in.

The roof above me was made of woven leaves, while light-colored wood twisted around to form an oval shape, making up the walls. A beautifully crafted bay window overlooked a glittering ocean. We obviously weren't on the ship. Nor the horrible frozen land to the north.

The sound of footsteps coming up the spiral staircase alerted me to Fallon's approach.

"Rabbit, you're awake." His smile was warm, but his eyes held a stern look I didn't recognize.

I nodded, getting to my feet. A wave of dizziness threw me

off-kilter, and Fallon rushed to steady me before I fell. I took his hand for guidance as he led me down the stairs.

The first floor of the wooden home was oval-shaped as well. A large pool sat in the center of the room, with steam coming from it. It was lined with rocks that separated one steaming portion from the rest of the pool. I made a mental note to make full use of that at my earliest convenience.

Stepping outside, the dark of the night made it a little hard to see my surroundings, but the moon cast a beautiful illumination on the beach. A large pot was placed above a bonfire where delicious smells rolled off the top. The sea was like a glittering blanket of aquamarine gems. Calm waves lapped blissfully on the sandy shore as songbirds blasted their infernal tune, even at that hour. When I tuned them out, the sound of the waves was incredibly soothing.

Fallon's arms came around my waist, pulling me to his broad chest. "You said you wanted to come back to the island when our task was over. An entire month I believe it was?"

"I did say that." But that was before he went mad and cut a guy in half. I leaned back against his chest, inhaling his comforting scent. "How long have I been asleep, Fallon?"

The hands around me twitched. "Just a few days."

"Just a few days," I repeated. My eyes closed as I braced myself to ask a question I wasn't sure I wanted the answer to. "Did you go back and kill them?"

He was silent for a moment. "No," he growled out. "I wanted

to, but no." Relief eased the tension in my shoulders. "Then why keep me asleep?"

"I didn't…want you to see me that angry. Every time I thought about you almost getting run through by them, the rage I felt would be all-consuming. I wanted to kill everyone. So instead, I used the magic I stole from Myva to bring you here and build things for our stay." He leaned down and kissed my head before releasing me. "Come, I cooked you sea spiders."

"Sea spiders?" I said, raising a brow.

He grinned. A bit of that playful demeanor I'd come to adore returned to his face. "I don't know what they're called. I've only flown over the ocean before, never hunted from it —but they look and smell similar to your crawfish." He pulled back the lid of the pot to reveal crab legs. He'd recreated the same crawfish boil I showed him our first night in the bayou. "I wasn't sure what spices you used exactly, so I went by how they smelled when I grabbed ingredients from a village I passed through."

I groaned and buried my face in my hands. The beating of my heart felt like a war drum.

Fallon frowned and looked at the boiling pot. "Is it that bad?"

"No," I groaned out, grabbing a plate and piling it high. "It's just such a damn considerate and sweet thing to do. I don't know how to handle it." The fact that this man could go from cutting someone in half to cooking me one of my favorite dishes after building me a fucking beach house was too much to handle. The extremes of Fallon's love made my head spin. I made peace with the fact that I didn't hate it, as morally questionable as it was.

He let out a breath and made up his own plate. His long legs brushed up against mine as he sat next to me. We ate in silence for a while, just enjoying each other's company and the chance to be alone. As much as I wanted this moment to continue, I knew my demon well enough to know when he was keeping something from me. "You don't plan on letting me leave this island, do you." It was more of a statement than a question.

Fallon reached up to rub the nape of his neck. "I can keep you safe here." He gazed at the fire, avoiding my stare.

I took his hand in mine and scooted closer. "Fallon, I wasn't hurt."

"But you almost were!" he shouted. My demon stood and began to pace, no doubt trying to outrun whatever ill fate had befallen me in his head. "If I had been a second late, you would have been taken from me!"

"You weren't."

His gaze snapped to me. There was such pain and devotion in his dark eyes, it made my chest squeeze. "Cin, I can barely breathe when you are not near. If anything were to happen to you, if you left me to be alone again, these memories of you would kill me."

He took a step back as I approached him. I reached up to

cup his face, pressing my body against his in reassurance. He shivered. The fear he must have felt from spending so many years alone showed through. It was no wonder he went slightly mad with it.

"I love you too."

His hand came to rest on the small of my back. The touch was so gentle it was barely a whisper.

"But I won't live in a beautiful cage."

"Not forever," he said desperately. "Just until you gain control of your magic and can protect yourself."

"You said that would take years."

"Did you see the heated bath in the house?" His chest shook as he tried to force out a laugh. "I can give you anything. Just say the word, and it's yours," he whispered.

I closed my eyes and kissed him. His arms came around me, squeezing so tight it was hard to breathe for a moment. "Fallon, you're going to have to trust me."

"I can't." His hand snaked up the nape of my neck to take hold of my curls, trapping me to him. He tilted my head back and kissed my throat. "Please." His voice came out hot and ragged.

"Can you truly make me anything?"

"Yes," he said quickly, hope blooming in his eyes. "With that lich's magic, I have enough power to make damn near anything."

"Then can't you just make me a protective shield like she

had on her temples? I understand it didn't affect humans, but couldn't you modify it if that's what you are afraid of?"

His movements stilled. The crackle of fire filled the pause in the air. "I'm a fucking idiot."

I let out a giggle. The tension from Fallon's shoulders slipped away beneath my hands. "So we're good?"

"Yes." My demon held me in a tight embrace. "But it will take time to figure out. Possibly a few months."

"I don't mind an extended honeymoon." I reached his mouth and kissed him passionately until he surrendered with a groan. He answered in kind, possessively claiming my touch as if he'd die without it. I pulled away, panting, my body aching with want. "So, are we going to break in that new bed or what?"

Fallon blinked down at me. His hand came up to caress my cheek. "You are my heart."

He grabbed me by the waist and hauled me over his shoulder. I yelped in surprise when he smacked my ass and took off into the house. Grinning ridiculously, I braced myself against Fallon's muscular back as he rushed up the stairs.

With a stomp of his foot, torches placed around the room lit up in a blaze. I gasped as sparkles of ember danced in the night air. The handsome features of my demon became apparent as he lowered me onto the bed. He stared at me with such hunger I thought I'd burst into flames myself.

"My wife," he whispered before capturing my lips in a

tender kiss that felt so right, so perfect. I melted into him. He nipped at my lower lip, then drove his tongue into me, tasting all I had to give him. I loved the greedy and possessive way Fallon touched me. It made me feel like a feast set in front of a starving man. He kissed his way down my neck, pausing only to dispose of my clothes. And by that, I mean he tore my blouse off like it personally offended him. I gasped and fixed him with a glare as he threw my ruined blouse behind him.

Fallon only chuckled and sank to his knees in front of the bed. "I'll make you new clothes. In a week or so." My skirt and undergarments were the next to feel his vendetta. He shredded them instantly, leaving me bare for him.

"You're just going to have me run around naked on this island?" I asked.

Fallon rubbed his hands up my thighs before running his tongue along the sensitive skin there, making me shiver. "Of course not. I'm not a monster." He paused his movements to glance up at me. "You can have a towel."

"My, how sweet of you."

A low, sinful murmur from Fallon caressed the sensitive skin of my inner thigh. "I am the epitome of benevolence." A grin tugged at the corner of his mouth before I broke out into a laugh. His hands gripped my hips and pulled me forward, presenting my core to him. My heart pounded in anticipation as his warm breath fanned over my pussy. I gasped as he gave it a long lick before dipping his tongue into my entrance. My hands crushed the soft blankets beneath me as he kissed and sucked on my clit.

"Oh Gods, that's good," I whispered before grabbing on to his horns. Fallon moaned into me as his rough hands pulled my thighs further apart. He drove his tongue deeper into me, eating me as I desperately tried to rock against his face. My body needed him like I needed air to breathe. The magic stored in my veins seeped out to greet him. His own dark mist rolled into the room like a storm brewing.

He gave another long lick to my pussy before pushing a finger into me. "I can finally get my fill of you," he groaned. "I'm going to keep you here, naked and ready for me, until my essence is burned into every part of you."

Sparks danced across my skin as his finger brushed against my sweet spot. "That is, without question, the best idea you've ever had."

Fallon tightened his grip against my ass before sucking harshly on my clit. His finger curved into my sweet spot, making me scream.

My eyes rolled into the back of my head. "Ahhh!" My orgasm swept me up in a riptide. It was suffocating in its intensity, but oh so fucking good. Fallon continued to pump his digit into me, drawing my pleasure out as long as he could. My legs locked around his head as I pleaded and begged for more. Anything. Everything that included his hands on me.

"I love you like this," he breathed before lifting me up

further on the bed. My demon moved on top of me. He trapped one of my wrists in his hand as the other traced the curve of my breasts. "Begging for me, your body trembling." A villainous grin spread over his face as his fingers, rough and long, focused on one of my sensitive nipples. "Does it ache, my love?" The feral, predatory glint in his eyes took on a satisfactory hue as my body arched up to him.

The sight of this beautiful, powerful man above me had me weak in the knees. He hissed as I stroked his cock with my free hand, guiding it to my entrance. I felt hollow, like a burning emptiness that needed filling. "Fallon, I need you."

He shuddered above me before taking the head of his cock and slowly rubbing it against the folds of my pussy. He stared down at me for a moment, as if to capture it in time. With a grunt, he thrust deep into me. I gasped as I stretched around him, trying to accommodate the delicious invasion. He closed his eyes and moved again, burying himself fully. Fallon let out a groan as I clenched around his cock. "This damn cunt is going to ruin me, Cinnamon."

I quivered beneath him as he pulled out and shoved his cock in again. My breath came out in desperate moans as he lifted my hips higher, allowing him to grind slow and deep against my sweet spot. My toes curled as need coiled in the pit of my belly. The pace was maddening. Fallon brushed against my desires in sweet torture. My free hand clawed at his back, urging him faster. He chuckled and lowered his head to whisper in my ear. "I know, little Rabbit. Slow and sweet just doesn't give you what you need, does it?" He ran his tongue along my neck as he kept his slow grinding pace. I spread my legs wider, trying to buck against him.

Embarrassment colored my cheeks. *Of course, I fell for a man who relishes teasing me.* "You know what I want."

Fallon nipped at my ear before giving a harder thrust, making me gasp. "And you know I want to hear you say it." He pulled away to look at my face. His sinful grin did all kinds of evil things to my heart. "Tell me what you want, Rabbit."

My nerves came alive under his gaze, the walls of my pussy clenched around him as if to demand I give in, just to release the burning need I felt.

*Pride is stupid anyway.*

"I want you to flip me over and fuck me senseless. I want your hand grabbing my neck as you spank me until I come. Then I want you to pull my hair as you rut into me. And I want it now."

The look on his face was almost comical. Fallon's mouth hung open for a moment before snapping it shut. "I love you," he whispered.

"I know," I said, nodding. "Now flip me over and tell me I'm a good girl."

The world spun as Fallon did as he was told, dragging my knees up and pushing my head down into the pillows. He ran a hand along the soft skin on my ass before smacking it. I cried out as he plunged balls deep into my pussy. He groaned out intoxicating words of praise while rutting into me at a brutal pace. His hand came around my neck, choking me slightly as he drove deeper. My hands clawed at the bed as the sound of my ass slapping against him played a magnificent sonnet in my ears.

"You are so beautiful," Fallon moaned, smacking my ass again. My back arched, another orgasm ripping through me as his cock ruined my body.

My hips thrust back in time with him, trying to steal as much wretched corruption as he was willing to offer. "Please don't stop," I sobbed. His hand left my throat to grip my hips tighter. "Yes! Please, please fuck me."

"Gods, you know I love it when you beg." His nails dug into my hips, the sharp sting of pain heightening my pleasure as the force of his cock thundering into me drove me to the edge of euphoria once more. Fallon slowly pulled out to drag the head of his cock against my clit, before slamming himself back in. My head threw back as I screamed his name. He ground deep into me before pulling out and slamming in a few more times. The savage pace made me see stars as I continued to shout his name.

My orgasm was so violent, I thought I might die for a moment. This time, when my body clenched around him, Fallon broke. He emptied his cock inside me with a grunt. He thrust into me a few more times before collapsing onto his side, bringing me with him.

His muscular chest heaved heavily against my back as I tried to remember my own name. I curled up against him, body still shaking with the after tremors of my orgasm. He wrapped a muscular arm around my waist and buried his head in my hair. The magic in the room faded, melting back into us like a cup of cocoa on a chill winter day. Tears pricked my eyes at the tenderness of the moment. The wave of devotion and warmth from our bond had my mind in a tizzy. "I love you," I said, stroking his hand.

Fallon kissed my shoulder. "I love you too."

I sighed in contentment as the exhaustion set in. "How long do you think before Usha comes crashing in with the crew?"

"I put up signs directing her to the other side of the island. If she ignores them, I'm burning the damn ship down."

Laughter bubbled out of my throat. "You didn't!"

"Intruders will catch these flames." He held me closer, grinning against my shoulder as I fell into a fit of giggles.

# Epilogue

It was nearly the end of the harvest season. Colorful leaves were scattered from the trees all over cobblestone roads. Fallon pulled my scarf higher above my nose as we walked down a familiar trail. His red pendant gleamed against my chest with solid protective magic. The piece of gaudy jewelry was the only reason my overprotective spouse had agreed to let us leave the safety of our island—though spending three months in paradise was far from a difficult task.

We moved through the winding streets of Boohail until the smell of our cinnamon fields greeted me like an old friend. My heart sped up as my parents' home came into view. Grabbing Fallon's hand, I ran to it, damn near tripping over my own two feet in excitement. My demon laughed at my antics but sped up all the same.

Without warning, I burst open the door. My pa and both my brothers sat at the table while Ma approached with a plate of food. Their gazes snapped to us in surprise.

"I'm home!" I pulled Fallon in after me, forcing him to lower his head so his horns wouldn't scrape against the door frame. "Also, we're married, and the fake goddess is dead!"

Ma slammed her dish on the table before tackling me into her arms. Tears fell from my eyes as I hugged her back.

Fallon stepped aside to let us hug it out before turning to my father and brothers. "Hello again. Good to see you."

Pa got up from his chair slowly. "Wait, go back. Did she just say you were married?"

Chili was next to pipe up. "Your daughter just said she killed a goddess, and that's what you grab on to?"

Ma released me and wiped the tears from her eyes before wrapping Fallon in a fierce hug. He looked startled for a moment before gently hugging the crying woman back. "You brought her home. That's all I care about." She backed away, smiling. Cumin and Chili snapped out of their stupor to give me a hug.

Ma rushed over to the table, pulling out two more chairs. "Come sit!" she demanded. "Tell us everything."

The story continues in…

**_THAT TIME I GOT DRUNK AND YEETED_**
**_A LOVE POTION AT A WEREWOLF_**

Book TWO of the Mead Mishaps series

# Acknowledgments

Thank you, Alexis, Blair, Kiran, Rebekah, and Sabrina. You ladies gave me the courage to change everything and try something new, and I hope you know how much that means to me. You are without a shadow of a doubt, some of the best friends I've ever had.

# extras

orbit

# meet the author

Kimberly Lemming

KIMBERLY LEMMING is on an eternal quest to avoid her calling as a main character. She can be found giving the slip to that new werewolf that just blew into town and refusing to make eye contact with a prince of a far-off land. Dodging aliens looking for Earth booty can really take up a girl's time. But when she's not running from fate, she can be found writing diverse fantasy romance. Or just shoveling chocolate in her maw until she passes out on the couch.

Find out more about Kimberly Lemming and other Orbit authors by registering for the free monthly newsletter at orbitbooks.net.

# if you enjoyed

## THAT TIME I GOT DRUNK AND SAVED A DEMON

### look out for

# THE UNDERTAKING OF HART AND MERCY

### by

## Megan Bannen

*Hart Ralston is a marshal, tasked with patrolling the strange and magical wilds of Tanria. It's an unforgiving job, and he's got nothing but time to ponder his loneliness.*

*Mercy Birdsall never has a moment to herself. She's been single-handedly keeping Birdsall & Son, Undertakers, afloat in defiance of sullen jerks like Hart-ache Hart, who seems to have a gift for showing up right when her patience is thinnest.*

*After yet another exasperating run-in with Merciless Mercy, Hart
finds himself penning a letter addressed simply to "a friend."
Much to his surprise, an anonymous letter comes back in return,
and a tentative friendship is born.*

*If only Hart knew he's been baring his soul to the person who
infuriates him most—Mercy. As the dangers from Tanria grow
closer, so do the unlikely correspondents. But can their blossoming
romance survive the fated discovery that their pen pals are their
worst nightmares—each other?*

# Chapter One

It was always a gamble, dropping off a body at Birdsall & Son,
Undertakers, but this morning, the Bride of Fortune favored
Hart Ralston.

Out of habit, he ducked his head as he stepped into the
lobby so that he wouldn't smack his forehead on the doorframe.
Bold-colored paintings of the death gods—the Salt Sea, the
Warden, and Grandfather Bones—decorated the walls in gold
frames. Two green velvet armchairs sat in front of a walnut coffee
table, their whimsical lines imbuing the room with an upbeat
charm. Vintage coffee bean tins served as homes for pens and
candy on a counter that was polished to a sheen. This was not
the somber, staid lobby of a respectable place like Cunningham's
Funeral Services. This was the appalling warmth of an undertaker who welcomed other people's deaths with open arms.

It was also blessedly empty, save for the dog draped over one of the chairs. The mutt was scratching so furiously at his ribs he didn't notice that his favorite Tanrian Marshal had walked through the front door. Hart watched in delight as the mongrel's back paw sent a cyclone of dog hair whirling through a shaft of sunlight before the bristly fur settled on the velvet upholstery.

"Good boy, Leonard," said Hart, knowing full well that Mercy Birdsall did not want her dog wallowing on the furniture.

At the sound of his name, Leonard perked up and wagged his nubbin tail. He leaped off the chair and hurled himself at Hart, who petted him with equal enthusiasm.

Leonard was an ugly beast—half boxer, half the gods knew what, brindle coated, eyes bugging and veined, jowls hanging loose. In any other case, this would be a face only his owner could love, but there was a reason Hart continued to patronize his least favorite undertaker in all the border towns that clung to the hem of the Tanrian Marshals' West Station like beggar children. After a thorough round of petting and a game of fetch with the tennis ball Leonard unearthed from underneath his chair, Hart pulled his watch out of his vest pocket and, seeing that it was already late in the afternoon, resigned himself to getting on with his job.

He took a moment to doff his hat and brush back his overgrown blond hair with his fingers. Not that he cared how he looked. Not at Birdsall & Son, at any rate. As a matter of fact, if he had been a praying man, he would have begged the Mother of Sorrows to have mercy on him, no pun intended. But he was not entirely a man—not by half—much less one of the praying variety, so he left religion to the dog.

"Pray for me, Leonard," he said before he pinged the counter bell.

"Pop, can you get that?" Mercy's voice called from somewhere in the bowels of Birdsall & Son, loudly enough so that her father should be able to hear her but softly enough that she wouldn't sound like a hoyden shouting across the building.

Hart waited.

And waited.

"I swear," he muttered as he rang the bell again.

This time, Mercy threw caution to the wind and hollered, "Pop! The bell!" But silence met this request, and Hart remained standing at the counter, his impatience expanding by the second. He shook his head at the dog. "Salt fucking Sea, how does your owner manage to stay in business?"

Leonard's nubbin started up again, and Hart bent down to pet the ever-loving snot out of the boxer mix.

"I'm so sorry," Mercy said, winded, as she rushed from the back to take her place behind the counter. "Welcome to Birdsall & Son. How can I help you?"

Hart stood up—and up and up—towering over Mercy as her stomach (hopefully) sank down and down.

"Oh. It's you," she said, the words and the unenthusiastic tone that went with them dropping off her tongue like a lead weight. Hart resisted the urge to grind his molars into a fine powder.

"Most people start with *hello*."

"Hello, Hart-ache," she sighed.

"Hello, Merciless." He gave her a thin, venomous smile as he took in her oddly disheveled appearance. Whatever else he might say about her, she was usually neat as a pin, her bright-colored dresses flattering her tall, buxom frame, and her equally bright lipstick meticulously applied to her full lips. Today, however, she wore overalls, and her olive skin was dewy with sweat, making her red horn-rimmed glasses slide down her nose. A couple of dark curls had come loose from the floral scarf that bound up her hair, as if she'd stuck her head out the window while driving full speed across a waterway.

"I guess you're still alive, then," she said flatly.

"I am. Try to contain your joy."

Leonard, who could not contain his joy, jumped up to paw Hart's stomach, and Hart couldn't help but squeeze those sweet jowls in his hands. What a shame that such a great dog belonged to the worst of all undertaking office managers.

"Are you here to pet my dog, or do you actually have a body to drop off?"

A shot of cold humiliation zinged through Hart's veins, but he'd never let her see it. He held up his hands as if Mercy were leveling a pistol crossbow at his head, and declared with mock innocence, "I stopped by for a cup of tea. Is this a bad time?"

Bereft of adoration, Leonard leaped up higher, mauling Hart's ribs.

"Leonard, get down." Mercy nabbed her dog by the collar to drag him upstairs to her apartment. Hart could hear him scratching at the door and whining piteously behind the wood. It was monstrous of Mercy to deprive both Hart and her dog of each other's company. Typical.

"Now then, where were we?" she said when she returned, propping her fists on her hips, which made the bib of her overalls stretch over the swell of her breasts. The square of denim seemed to scream, *Hey, look at these! Aren't they fucking magnificent?* It was so unfair of Mercy to have magnificent breasts.

"You're dropping off a body, I assume?" she asked.

"Yep. No key."

"Another one? This is our third indigent this week."

"More bodies mean more money for you. I'd think you'd be jumping for joy."

"I'm not going to dignify that with a response. I'll meet you at the dock. You do know there's a bell back there, right?"

"I prefer the formality of checking in at the front desk."

"Sure you do." She rolled her eyes, and Hart wished they'd roll right out of her unforgivably pretty face.

"Does no one else work here? Why can't your father do it?"

Like a gift from the Bride of Fortune, one of Roy Birdsall's legendary snores galloped through the lobby from behind the thin wall separating it from the office. Hart smirked at Mercy, whose face darkened in embarrassment.

"I'll meet you at the dock," she repeated through gritted teeth.

Hart's smirk came with him as he put on his hat, sauntered out to his autoduck, and backed it up to the dock.

"Are you sure you're up for this?" he asked Mercy as he swung open the door of his duck's cargo hold, knowing full well that she would find the question unbearably condescending.

As if to prove that she didn't need anyone's help, least of all his, she snatched the dolly from its pegs on the wall, strode past him into the hold, and strapped the sailcloth-wrapped body to the rods with the practiced moves of an expert. Unfortunately, this particular corpse was extremely leaky, even through the thick canvas. Despite the fact that he had kept it on ice, the liquid rot wasn't completely frozen over, and Mercy wound up smearing it all over her hands and arms and the front of her overalls. Relishing her horror as it registered on her face, Hart sidled up to her, his tongue poking into the corner of his cheek. "I don't want to say I told you so, but—"

She wheeled the corpse past him, forcing him to step out of the autoduck to make room for her. "Hart-ache, if you don't want my help, maybe you should finally find yourself a partner."

The insinuation lit his Mercy Fuse, which was admittedly short. As if he would have any trouble finding a partner if he wanted one. Which he didn't.

"I didn't ask for your help," he shot back. "And look who's talking, by the way."

She halted the dolly and pulled out the kickstand with the toe of her sneaker. "What's that supposed to mean?"

"It means I don't see anyone helping you either." He fished inside his black vest for the paperwork she would need to complete in order to receive her government stipend for processing the body, and he held it out to her. He had long since learned to have his end all filled out ahead of time so that he didn't have to spend a second longer in her presence than was necessary.

She wiped one hand on the clean fabric over her ass before snatching the papers out of his hand. Without the consent of his reason, Hart's own hands itched with curiosity, wondering exactly how the round curves of her backside would feel in his grasp. His brain was trying to shove aside the unwanted lust when Mercy stepped into him and stood on her tiptoes. Most women couldn't get anywhere near Hart's head without the assistance of a ladder, but Mercy was tall enough to put her into kissing range when she stood on the tips of her red canvas shoes. Her big brown eyes blazed behind the lenses of her glasses, and the unexpected proximity of her whole body felt bizarrely intimate as she fired the next words into his face.

"Do you know what I think, Hart-ache?"

He swallowed his unease and kept his voice cool. "Do tell, Merciless."

"You must be a pathetically friendless loser to be this much of a jerk." On the word *jerk*, she poked him in the chest with the emphatic pointer finger of her filthy hand, dotting his vest with brown rot and making him stumble onto the edge of the dock. Then she pulled down the gate before he could utter another word, letting it slam shut between them with a resounding *clang*.

Hart stood teetering on the lip of the dock in stunned silence. Slowly, insidiously, as he regained his balance, her words seeped beneath his skin and slithered into his veins.

*I will never come here again unless I absolutely have to*, he promised himself for the hundredth time. Birdsall & Son was not the only official drop-off site for bodies recovered in Tanria without ID tags. From now on, he would take his keyless cadavers to Cunningham's. But as he thought the words, he knew they constituted a lie. Every time he slayed an indigent drudge in Tanria, he brought the corpse to Birdsall & Son, Undertakers.

For a dog.

Because he was a pathetically friendless loser.

He already knew this about himself, but the fact that Mercy knew it, too, made his spine bunch up. He got into his auto-duck and drove to the station, his hands white-knuckling the wheel as he berated himself for letting Mercy get to him.

Mercy, with her snotty *Oh. It's you.* As if a dumpster rat had waltzed into her lobby instead of Hart.

Mercy, whose every word was a thumbtack spat in his face, pointy end first.

The first time he'd met her, four years ago, she had walked into the lobby, wearing a bright yellow dress, like a jolt of sunlight bursting through glowering clouds on a gloomy day. The large brown eyes behind her glasses had met his and widened, and he could see the word form in her mind as she took in the color of his irises, as pale and colorlessly gray as the morning sky on a cloudy day.

*Demigod.*

Now he found himself wondering which was worse: a pretty young woman seeing him as nothing more than the offspring of a divine parent, or Merciless Mercy loathing him for the man he was.

## Follow us:

**f** **/orbitbooksUS**

**X** **/orbitbooks**

**▶** **/orbitbooks**

Join our mailing list
to receive alerts on our
latest releases and deals.

**orbitbooks.net**

Enter our monthly
giveaway for the chance
to win some epic prizes.

**orbitloot.com**